out of my dreams

ALSO BY SHARON M. DRAPER

The Out of My Mind Series

Out of My Mind

Out of My Heart

The Clubhouse Mysteries

The Buried Bones Mystery

Lost in the Tunnel of Time

Shadows of Caesar's Creek

The Space Mission Adventure

The Backyard Animal Show

Stars and Sparks on Stage

Other Novels

Battle of Jericho

Blended

Copper Sun

Darkness Before Dawn

Double Dutch

Forged by Fire

Just Another Hero

November Blues

Panic

Romiette and Julio

Stella by Starlight

Tears of a Tiger

out of my dreams

SHARON M. DRAPER

A Caitlyn Dlouhy Book
ATHENEUM BOOKS FOR YOUNG READERS
atheneum   New York   London   Toronto   Sydney   New Delhi

ATHENEUM BOOKS FOR YOUNG READERS • An imprint of Simon & Schuster Children's Publishing Division • 1230 Avenue of the Americas, New York, New York 10020 • This book is a work of fiction. Any references to historical events, real people, or real places are used fictitiously. Other names, characters, places, and events are products of the author's imagination, and any resemblance to actual events or places or persons, living or dead, is entirely coincidental. • Text © 2024 by Sharon M. Draper • Jacket illustration © 2024 by Daniel Egnéus • Jacket photography (sky) by vecteezy/iStock • Jacket Photoshop work by Steve Gardner • Jacket design by Debra Sfetsios-Conover • All rights reserved, including the right of reproduction in whole or in part in any form. • ATHENEUM BOOKS FOR YOUNG READERS is a registered trademark of Simon & Schuster, LLC. • Atheneum logo is a trademark of Simon & Schuster, LLC. • Simon & Schuster: Celebrating 100 Years of Publishing in 2024 • For information about special discounts for bulk purchases, please contact Simon & Schuster Special Sales at 1-866-506-1949 or business@simonandschuster.com. • The Simon & Schuster Speakers Bureau can bring authors to your live event. For more information or to book an event, contact the Simon & Schuster Speakers Bureau at 1-866-248-3049 or visit our website at www.simonspeakers.com. • The text for this book was set in ITC New Baskerville Std. • Manufactured in the United States of America • 0724 BVG • First Edition • 10 9 8 7 6 5 4 3 2 1 • Library of Congress Control Number: 2024938226 • ISBN 9781665949545 • ISBN 9781665949569 (ebook)

This book is for
Damon Draper and David Brantley Jr.,
whose chances to dream
and fly were cut short.

out of my dreams

CHAPTER 1

I walked to the podium, tall and confident. I wore a dusky-red velvet dress that swirled lightly with each step I took. A black silk sash and satiny-smooth shoes completed the look.

I turned to the crowd and waved. I could hear cheers, yes, cheers, for me, Melody Brooks!

"We love ya, Melody!"

"You're the best, Melody!"

"We are so proud of you, Melody!"

"Can't wait to hear from you!"

I smiled brightly, acknowledging each person as I

passed them. Mom and Dad and Penny were in the front row, and near them I spotted our neighbors Mrs. V and Miss Gertie, and a girl I didn't recognize. And ooh, was that Noah from camp? OMG! My heart skipped a beat. I couldn't believe he showed up!

Reaching the podium, I grabbed both sides, lifted my chin, and took a deep breath. I spoke loudly and clearly, my voice echoing from the microphone.

"To all my friends and relatives who have gathered here today, I am so very thankful. And to all of you who don't know the full story of how a surprise trip changed my life and opened new doors for me, here we go!"

More applause. Was that music playing in the background? I felt like dancing. My feet wiggled in my shoes, and suddenly I was tipping, tapping, twirling across the stage to the beautiful strains of a soft Strauss waltz. So I danced. Yes, I danced. Right there onstage in front of hundreds of people. The notes and the melody did their own dance in my heart, just like my name. I glided across the stage as lightly as the golden air around me. Music raised me up as I reached for the sky. I stretched, farther, farther, and then . . .

I opened my eyes, as the dream began to crumble into the reality of morning, I realized I could not speak; there was no music, not even any random birds squawking outside.

I was in my bed, waiting for my mom to get me up, place me in my wheelchair, and get me ready for the day, which would not, for sure, include dancing!

But what a strange dream. . . .

CHAPTER 2

**Fully awake now, I gazed out my bedroom window—
I'd fallen asleep propped up on my pillows, so at least
I could see outside—but my view was gray, gray, and
more gray. Not one peek of blue sky among the, yep,
thick gray clouds. It had been raining all night, so brown
puddles muddied our lawn. Even the leaves hung list-
lessly, heavy with water droplets.**

Thunder rumbled in the distance. Thunder used to
spook me, but now it reminded me of being at camp
earlier this summer, where during art class, I learned
how to use the thick, gloppy paint to express my feelings, especially the harder ones like when I was confused

or hurt. If I were painting now, my page would be filled with browns and grays and dirty blues. I shivered and looked around for a sweatshirt—there was a dark orange one at the foot of my bed, but I couldn't put it on by myself, or get out of my pj's. Ugh.

I was stuck looking out the window till Mom showed up.

Each raindrop became a tiny explosion against the ground. I doubt if anyone can hear just one raindrop, but hundreds of them make their own kind of music. It's rhythmic, yet gray. I can usually sense a color in just about everything. For example, the rustling of leaves sounds like green, and the wind in my hair feels like blue, and my favorite cookies taste like gold. But I didn't sense colors in today's rain.

And I still didn't hear one single bird chirping. Did birds run for cover in a storm? It must be hard, with only leaves or skinny branches to stay dry under. But maybe they liked rainy days—free showers!

And the wind—wow. It was seriously spooky outside. And there were certainly no crowds in an audience waiting to hear me give a speech!

Maybe it was the world's way of crying with me and every other kid—summer vacation was nearly over. As if in answer, lightning sparked across the sky.

At least I was safe and warm inside. The storm could do the painting in gray droplets. Soaked, saturated, sodden, full of spurts and splashes. Ha! All the words that just slid out of my mind began with the letter *S*. I have this unspoken love affair with words, maybe because I can't actually speak them. My words are like bubbles from under the sea, floating around me, floating within me, silent, screaming to be heard. At the same time, words make me whole. Which is ironic because, hello, I can't talk.

But that doesn't shut me up. So don't be feeling sorry for me. Because I have a lot to say.

CHAPTER 3

Here's the thing. Lots of people talk who have nothing to say. But for me, words are my superpower—I use them to fly me to galaxies of understanding, to joke around with friends at a picnic table, or to tell my little sister, Penny, to open the back door so that our dog, Butterscotch, can go out and pee.

Lucky for me, I've got a device that helps me get the words out, a computerlike machine called a Medi-Talker. Just by touching a few squares with my right thumb (it behaves best!), it talks for me—and full sentences emerge. I named it Elvira—the device, not my thumb—ha-ha. Why? "'Cause I can," Penny would sass.

Actually, it's from an old song Dad always plays in the car.

Before Elvira, which sits on a specially made shelf on the side of my bed at night, I had a zillion thoughts stuck in my head with no way to get them out. But now I can have ordinary conversations with my family and the new friends I made at camp. I just wish the voice installed in it didn't sound like a kid with a really bad cold. In my head, I'm thinking I should sound like Beyoncé.

Maybe they'll fix it one day. Maybe I will!

A few weeks ago at Camp Green Glades, I also got to do other kinds of things I had never even dreamed of. Gee, I loved that camp! Truth? I didn't think I would when I first got there. I was scared, away from home for the first time ever, and way out of my comfort zone. Like, duh—I can't walk or talk and you want me to go to camp and hike through the woods? But it ended up being the best thing ever, even when we ran into a skunk! I'm usually transported by a wheelchair, but at camp I rode a horse—in a thunderstorm—by myself!! Well, it wasn't exactly supposed to happen like that, but even though I ended up soaking wet and totally terrified, I had a blast. Plus, I went zip-lining—yep, me—hung out under the stars around a blazing campfire, and even learned to swim. It was the most fun I'd had in my entire life.

Even better? For the first time, I made friends. I glanced down at my skinny wrist and gently touched the frayed, multicolored friendship bracelet that my friends and I wore at camp. It was really the first time in my life that I'd ever had anyone my age to giggle and whisper with. Ever.

The four of us have sent a few texts to each other since then, but nothing is as awesome as singing songs by a blazing campfire.

That might sound like no big deal, but, for real? Before I went to camp, I never had one single person who I could call a real friend. Yeah, I knew kids at school, but no one actually wanted to hang around with me, not even for a minute. A lot of them, well, didn't even seem to see me. They'd walk around me. Or pretend I was invisible. Guess what that made me feel like? Yeah, invisible.

But at camp—all the kids had some sort of challenge, which is how I guess the rest of the world sees us. There were kids who had spina bifida, and Down syndrome, and some conditions I'd never heard of. We all needed help, just in different ways. And because we *all* got help, it all started to feel . . . normal. Weird, huh? For one magical week, we felt ordinary. We slept in cabins, ate our meals together, went to our first dance together, and almost got sprayed by a skunk together—actually, a few kids did get sprayed! Yeah, friendship. I could hardly wait until next summer.

Until then, I was back to pre-camp normal, which

was not very normal at all. The condition that I've been labeled with is called cerebral palsy. Isn't that an awful-sounding name? Maybe I should start a campaign to name it something more interesting or funny, like spaghetti legs or noodle toes. For now, it is what it is, but it's not who I AM.

But what it meant was, in a few weeks, I would have to return to a school where the kids who are used to me will ignore me, and the new kids are gonna stare for sure at the seventh-grade girl who rolls down the halls in a motorized wheelchair. (I'd give anything to make it go faster!) I'm the only kid who had to be fed (yep, it's embarrassing) and who needed help to go to the bathroom. Double embarrassing!

I'm the kid whose mouth hangs open sometimes—and the drool is its own situation! Oof. I'm the one whose arms fling out unexpectedly, whose legs are toothpick-skinny in slightly cute stretch pants, whose shoes are always scuff-free on the bottom.

That's what they see. They don't see *me*. Melody Brooks. I can do eleventh-grade algebra problems in my head. Crossword puzzles too! I used to be in the special needs class because of my various "issues," but the school finally realized I'm supersmart, so they bounce me around, never quite sure where I belong. My math classes are all advanced level, which I ace, but I already know that my "hands-on" science course this year is going to be a challenge—probably more for the teacher than for me. One of the experiments will be slicing open a tomato to see what's inside, which is easy enough for kids who can hold a knife in one hand and the tomato in the other. For me, well . . . I feel sorry for the tomato!

I love golden retrievers and snowflakes. I like to visit the lions and tigers at the zoo. They're strong and powerful, yet somehow sad because they're limited by fences and cages. I totally get it.

I'm scared of bears—not sure why, because I never met one! And I don't like skunks—it's not their fault, but their smell is unforgettably, horribly funky. Let's just say I now know from experience!

I love bubbles. Yep, the thin, iridescent orbs that my little sister loves to chase. Bubbles are weightless and free—like dreams. What must that be like? Not tied down to the earth by gravity, or by disability?

I don't like chocolate, and that might be rarer than cerebral palsy! But I love words, even though I've never said a coherent one in my life. Like I said, I'm so lucky to have Elvira.

As I waited for my mom, and for the storm to pass, I noticed a flash of royal blue landing on my windowsill. It was one of Mrs. V's blue jays. Well, they're not *her* birds, of course, but she looks out for them, leaving them seeds and suet and nesting materials. When I asked her why, she simply replied, "Their blue makes me happy! Besides, they're scrappy and tough like you, Melody."

Now I get the happy part—a jay had never landed on my windowsill before, and it made me instantly excited, like a slice of blue sky had broken through all that gray after all! Watching the blue jay reminds me of the nature series Dad likes to binge-watch. Blue jays are feisty and bossy and squawk-yell at each other. They steal twigs from each other's nests and gobble whatever food shows up each morning.

But hello—they eat ants! Even at my hungriest, I don't think I could handle an ant sandwich. The blue jay must have sensed my thoughts, because it flittered off, probably pecking at the suet from the feeder that Mrs. V had hung up in her backyard. It was kinda like a jaybird fast-food restaurant. I guess they'll eat ants for dessert. Then, after totally pigging out, they simply lift their wings and soar into the sky. Lucky blue jays!

Blue's my favorite color, by the way. It makes me feel calm and peaceful; it's the color I see when I close my eyes at night. But blue also burns brightly in the center of a flame!

Of course, just as I was thinking about peaceful blue and flying, the bird flittered back over toward me with a squawk, and . . . dropped a splat of poop on my window! And then I was cracking up. I'd have to tell Mrs. V about that one!

Mrs. V, whose full name is Violet Valencia, lives next door. She's practically like family. She helps my parents with me and Penny. She traveled around the world when she was younger, can speak three languages, has read hundreds of books, and does a full yoga workout every morning. She hasn't missed a day in five years, she told me.

And Mrs. V was the one who first opened my life to speech and actual conversation. She was the one who pushed me to stretch, to defy boundaries, and to succeed when I had no idea I could do any of it. She was even the one who found Elvira for me! Mrs. V never sees anything impossible in my life—only possibilities.

I already knew what she'd say if I asked her about blue jays: "Let's look this up. Let's do some research. Let's find some photos."

By "let's," she means me. So that was what I did. Elvira is also a fully functional supercomputer, so I thought I might as well start researching blue jays while I was waiting for Mom. Hmm—blue jays eat all kinds of insects, and eggs robbed from other nests. They're pretty bird pirates!

And now I know why they strut about on Mrs. V's

lawn instead of hopping. They've got heavier legs and feet than most birds.

I was admiring close-ups of those cool crests on their heads—like they're all flying around with crowns on—when, at last, I heard Mom walking down the hall. Penny must have woken her up; she was chattering away about her latest passion—fingernail polish. She had bottles of the stuff all around the house—every color imaginable, and some I'm sure somebody just made up. So Mom got her a shiny red Caboodle to contain the mess—one of those plastic bins with a handle and little squares inside—and now Penny carries that thing everywhere. It's filled with pink frosted lip gloss, hair clips, kid cologne, and even body glitter. And yes, eight zillion bottles of nail polish! The part that's impressive is that she's not even five, but she knows exactly how to apply the polish—she never spills a drop. Her hands never shake or wobble as she paints her left hand with the right, and her right hand with her left. Her dexterity amazes me, and, facts, maybe makes me a *little* envious. I couldn't even hold a spoon long enough to feed myself without spilling. I glanced at the bird poop on my window—couldn't wipe that up either!

CHAPTER 4

Past my window, I saw—no one. The folks who live on our street are pretty predictable, and apparently avoid the rain, ha. Mr. and Mrs. Casselberry live in the big yellow house to the left of us. They wave sometimes as they walk their dogs—three miniature poodles. Butterscotch probably laughs as those little bitty dogs march down the street in matching outfits. Seriously, the last time it rained, they all wore cute tiny yellow doggie raincoats.

Across the street lives Miss Gertie. She's old. I mean old-old. I'm not being impolite—she just is! Her hair is silver, wrapped up in a bun . . . and she walks pretty slowly to her mailbox, then back, every day.

She's gotta be lonely, I figured, because I've hardly ever seen anyone visit her. Once in a while she sees me sitting in the window and gives a wave. In return, I flap my arms as hard as I can to wave back.

No wave today, I was thinking as Penny exploded into my room. My sister doesn't walk, she bursts, and her constant chatter sizzles with energy.

"Hey, Dee-Dee," she blurted out, thrusting a hand in front of me. "Which do you like better: the lavender and pink champagne polish?" Then she thrusts the other hand out. "Or this: the tangerine and buttercup yellow?" Then she began blowing on each finger.

Just so I didn't swing my arm out and accidentally smear her polish, I quickly typed, **"Buttercup!"**

Penny did a little happy dance, then darted out of the room—probably to watch her favorite show, *Yabba Dabba Duckie,* her mind and body racing to another adventure.

As I watched her run off, I felt so glad that she doesn't have to face the world from a wheelchair, that she can say whatever silliness pops into her mind, that she can paint her fingernails ten different colors if she wants to.

Mom peeked into my room. "Ready to get up, sleepyhead?"

Sleepyhead? Excuse me . . . I've been up with the birds! But I tapped **"Yes"** on my board and gave her a big smile, 'cause I try not to stress her. She's a nurse at the local hospital, and with her job plus seeing to all my needs, she doesn't get much rest. So I do my best to make things as easy as possible on my end.

Once we finished my morning bathroom business and getting dressed, she started breakfast. "You want your nails done too?" she asked.

I shook my head no vigorously; I wanted my camp polish to last as long as possible. It came with really good memories—the camp dance. And . . . Noah.

"Gotcha," she said with a smirk.

I tapped out the words, **"Penny is a whirlwind this morning. She's like a bubble dancing in the air."**

Mom raised an eyebrow knowingly. "You got that right!"

"Laughter like diamonds and sparkles of joy," I tapped next.

Mom ran her hand over my hair. "You have such a gift with words," she said. "You should write a book, maybe poetry."

I smiled. **"Maybe,"** I tapped. **"In my free time."**

We both laughed. She fed me one of my favorite breakfast meals—scrambled eggs drizzled with maple syrup. Hey, don't judge me! It's yummy!

"I'm gonna toss a load into the washer," she said, wheeling me back into my room and handing me my Dad-made custom TV channel changer. The buttons were as big as quarters; I could push them with my thumb so I didn't have to bother anybody when I needed to switch the station.

"Netflix?" Mom asked.

I shook my head. I'd seen just about every movie they had to offer. I could probably write a film script. Mom fiddled with the remote, then switched to the Disney Channel.

"What language?" she asked. She knew me so well.

"German," I tapped. She nodded, clicked it on the language setting, then handed me the remote.

I've started teaching myself other languages in addition to French, which I already knew: Spanish, Chinese, German, and Arabic. So I love watching shows in those languages whenever I can.

I settled into a movie about mountain climbers in the Himalayas. I might accomplish amazing things in my life, but inching up a mountain with just my fingertips and toes—nah, not gonna happen.

During a commerical I glanced out the window. Hey, the rain stopped. And there was Miss Gertie, dressed in a pale purple bathrobe, hands empty, walking away from her mailbox. When she reached the freshly blooming Tropicana roses lining her walkway, she paused, sniffed one.

Tropicanas (of course I'd researched them—lol!) are

usually a bright coral-orange color, but Miss Gertie must be some kind of rose whisperer—hers were pale pink, and orange sherbet. But her favorite was clearly a bush called the Peace rose. Its blooms were huge, golden, and edged in salmon. Miss Gertie watered that bush right down by the roots, sprinkled around little granules that I bet were fertilizer—and I know for sure she talked to it. I could see her whispering now as she pinched a random brown leaf from one of its stems.

As she straightened up and stretched her back, she saw me at the window. She waved and then pointed with pride at her blooms.

I flop-hand waved back.

She continued up the walkway. Suddenly, she seemed to stumble on something on the path. She pitched forward, swinging out her arms to steady herself. Maybe the walkway was slick because of the rain, or maybe she just couldn't catch her balance, but—oh no! She fell to the ground! I waited, heart thumping, for her to stir, to get back up, but she didn't seem to be moving.

I screeched for Mom, but she was in the basement doing laundry. I screeched for Penny. I screeched out to the empty air and closed windows of the neighborhood. Not one single car passed by. Not even a random blue jay. And Miss Gertie was lying motionless in her yard.

CHAPTER 5

I continued to holler for Mom, for Dad, for anybody!

Miss Gertie had not moved.

I could hear Mom singing as the washing machine chugged and sloshed. I could hear the beating of the water as Dad took his shower. Penny, deep into the latest episode of *Yabba Dabba Duckie*, had the sound up on full blast. No one could hear me.

Still, I hollered and hollered. Still not one car drove by. Not one neighbor jogged up the sidewalk. Where were the dog walkers? It was like a horrible movie scene, except this was real.

"Yabba Bo-dabba Duckieeeee!" came from the next room.

Chug-slosh, chug-slosh came from the laundry room.

I squealed and yelped and kicked. My legs do that, not that it helped.

Then it dawned on me—Elvira!

My heart began to flutter. I steadied my breathing, and, for the very first time ever, I tapped the 911-EMERGENCY square on the bottom left edge of my board.

A pleasant female voice picked up almost immediately. "911. What is your emergency?" I bet she had said that a thousand times.

My heart thumped. How could I possibly do this?

I took a deep breath, and hollered as loudly as I could, "Uhhhhh!"

The woman on the other end sighed loudly and repeated, "911. What is your emergency?"

I shrieked. When I get excited, my body control disappears, and my wobbly-bobbly moves go into overdrive.

"It is a crime to interfere with the work of the police and fire departments!" she almost barked at me. Then she hung up.

I was stunned. At the same time I couldn't blame her. I probably sounded like somebody who ought to be ignored. They probably get lots of prank calls at that job.

I hit the red button for the second time in my life. The same operator picked up. I let out another shriek.

"I will report you to my supervisors if you do this again!" She hung up again.

I redialed once more.

A male operator picked up this time. "911. What is your emergency?"

I tried again, this time grunting. "Uhhhhh!"

"This is an emergency line. Are you in an emergency situation?" The voice sounded annoyed.

Gahh! I probably sounded like a crazy person. Still, I screeched once more.

"Uhhhhh!" I was starting to panic. I couldn't think clearly.

"It is illegal to use this line to play games. Do you have an emergency?"

"Buhhhhh! Buhhhhh!"

The music of the duckie show blared in the background. Totally flustered, I glanced out the window. Miss Gertie hadn't moved an inch. And that's when I remembered the HELP tab on my talking board. Duh! How could I forget that? So I hit HELP on my board. Again and again.

"HELP! HELP! HELP! HELP!"

The operator kinda changed his tone then. "Can you speak?" he asked carefully.

I hit **"NO."** But I know that made no sense to him.

I tapped **"HELP"** once, twice more. I paused, took a breath, then took the time to tap out the words **"My name is Melody. Send help quick!"**

"Okay, Melody. Your voice doesn't sound normal. Can you tell me why?"

I had no time for explanations about my birth, my life, and all my issues. I tapped, **"HELP"** once more.

"Are you in trouble?" the operator asked at last.

Finally, I seemed to be getting through.

"Yes. Yes. Yes."

Now his voice shifted to all business. "Okay. My name is Jeffrey, and I'm going to try to help you."

At last! Took him long enough.

Jeffrey continued, now all in. "Your address has appeared on my screen. Are you in danger?"

How should I answer him? It wasn't me who was in danger. But I typed **"YES."**

"Are you hurt?" he asked.

"No. Friend."

"So your friend is in trouble?"

"YES!"

"Okay, I get it. I've just dispatched someone to your address. Let me ask you this, Melody: Are you using an assistive device?"

He got it! Thank God! Thank God! Thank God!

I tapped back quickly. **"YES! YES!"** I wondered how he knew, but I didn't want to take time to ask.

"Okay, I'm confirming that help is on the way!"

I felt a little like I was on one of those emergency rescue shows that Dad likes to watch. But this was real.

"Hurry!" I typed. **"My friend is hurt."**

"Is your friend with you?"

"No. Across the street."

"Are you safe?" he asked.

"Yes. I'm fine."

"Good. Tell me about your friend."

"She's reallllly old."

"Can you tell if she's breathing?"

"Can't tell." Then I tapped out, **"She fell. Hit her head. And she's still on the ground!"** Then I added, **"Her name is Miss Gertie."** It seemed to take forever to tap that out and hit send.

"This is terrific information," Jeffrey assured me. "I've passed it along to the crew."

I looked out the window once more, but still no one was in sight. I was thinking, *This Jeffrey guy sure is taking his sweet time to get this going!* To Miss Gertie, it must seem like a million years. Which is, if she was even conscious enough to be aware of how long she'd been on the ground. Which got me to worrying even more. What if she was unconscious? What if she was lying there and didn't even know it?

"Help is three minutes away," Jeffrey told me next. "You're doing a phenomenal job, Melody!"

I was thinking there was nothing magnificent about being nosy and checking out my neighbors, but I tapped, **"Thank you."**

It's so frustrating to be so slow to respond. My mind was racing at supersonic speed, but good old Elvira was only as fast as I could type. Which was stuck in mud level. Plus, while my machine is able to turn my thoughts into words, I don't think anybody has invented a system yet that can show feelings like fear or happiness or just plain terror.

Jeffrey kept on talking in a steady, soothing voice, probably trying to make sure I wasn't freaking out. Even though I already was!

"Do you have family nearby who you can contact?" he asked.

I took a deep breath. **"Dad is in the shower. Mom is doing laundry. My little sister is watching TV."**

This was taking forever!

"Is there any way you can contact your mom?" he asked.

"She's in the basement."

"Can you call out to your sister? How old is she?"

"Four and a half. She's watching her favorite show, really loud." I tapped as fast as I could.

Jeffrey almost chuckled—I could hear it—but I guess that wasn't appropriate for an emergency. So he simply said, "I've got a daughter about the same age. Is she watching that crazy *Yabba Dabba Duckie* show?"

How did he know? I tapped, **"Yep!"** It was a relief to type something quickly.

"Okay. Can you see out your window? Is Miss Gertie still on the ground?"

I checked. The sky was now streaked with blue; the grass emerald green, and Miss Gertie lay still by her roses.

"Yes! Hurry!" I tapped. **"Hurry!"**

Finally, I heard sirens in the distance.

CHAPTER 6

Penny burst into my room. "Look outside, Dee-Dee! There's an amboolance and sirens and police cars and wow!"

I tapped my board on a spot that Penny and I used a lot: **"GO GET MOM!"** Then added quickly, **"AND DAD!"**

Penny turned for the hallway, but Mom was already racing into my room.

"What's going on?" she asked. "Are you okay?"

"It's Miss Gertie," I tapped.

"Mom, look!" Penny said, her face now glued to my window. "Miss Gertie fell down. Look! It's so awesomely scary!"

A look of instant apprehension flashed across Mom's face. I've seen that look before. It's how grown-ups look when things are really bad, but they're trying to act like it's no big deal so the kids don't flip out.

An ambulance had stopped just short of Miss Gertie's flowers. A police cruiser was pulled up behind it. Blue-uniformed paramedics jumped out of the ambulance as a pair of cops raced over. I'm not sure if they were in competition to see who could get to Miss Gertie first, or if this was how it always looked at an emergency scene.

I hoped none of the big-booted emergency people stepped on her roses.

Jeffrey's voice came back. "The crews have arrived, Melody."

"Yes, yes! They're here!" I tapped back. **"Thank you! Thank you for being so fast!"**

"Don't thank me. It was *you*, Melody, who got help for Miss Gertie," Jeffrey said emphatically.

Me? I didn't do anything. I just made a phone call.

But Jeffrey was going on and on about how my call may well have saved somebody's life. Mom was staring from me to my board to me again, looking totally confused.

"If not for you, young lady, your neighbor would still be lying there! You are a hero, Melody!"

Now Mom's mouth fell open. She shot me a look of surprise.

A . . . what? I didn't feel heroic at all. I wasn't sure what that was even supposed to feel like.

Finally Jeffrey said, "I'm going to hang up now, okay? And hey, all of us here at the station are mighty proud of you!"

I tapped **"THANKS"** just as Dad ran into my room, smelling of his favorite "ocean breeze" soap.

"What's going on across the street?" he asked, drying his hair with a towel. "I heard sirens, and was afraid one of you guys was in trouble." He leaned down and kissed me on the forehead, tousled Penny's curls, then went over to the bird-pooped window.

"It's Miss Gertie." Mom's voice was full of concern.

"Oh boy. Is she okay? What happened?" He peered at the commotion across the street.

"She took a tumble on the walkway. Seems she must have hit her head," Mom told him. "I'm going to run over to see if I can be of any help—I'll be right back." A moment later she was dashing across our lawn, medical kit in hand.

"A fall at her age can be quite dangerous," Dad murmured. "Good thing someone called 911."

"It was Dee-Dee!" Penny announced with the power of a kid who gets to be the first to tell a tale.

"Melody?" Dad rubbed his hand over his head, looking at me. "But how?"

"Hit 911 on my board," I tapped.

"Smart thinking!" Dad said. He gave me a big hug. "Really smart thinking, honey!"

Then we were back to being plastered to the window. Across the street, Mom fit right in, not getting in the way, but offering assistance where she saw the need. I'd never actually seen her *working* as a nurse before. I wanted to tell everyone, *Hey, that's my mom out there!*

So many people hovered around Miss Gertie, two on their knees. She looked so tiny. A muscular paramedic was checking her heart with a stethoscope, while another one was opening a roll of gauze. This was scary real, nothing at all like on TV shows. There, the actors finished quickly and rushed the sick person away so the next scene could be shown in a hospital.

Here, a lady I actually knew was lying by a bed of roses, surrounded by so many medical professionals I couldn't even see her!

Mom suddenly scurried inside Miss Gertie's house. A moment later she emerged and handed one of the medics a purse and some cards—IDs and medical cards, maybe? I'd been in enough doctors' offices to know the importance of stuff like that.

Mom pointed to our house, then shook the officer's hand. She peeked over a kneeling paramedic's shoulder, nodded at something the woman said, then headed back down the walkway.

Finally, a stretcher was rolled up the walkway, and the paramedics gently moved Miss Gertie onto it. Once they strapped her in, they pressed a lever, and up the stretcher rose on its own. As they rolled her to the back of the ambulance, I saw a bandage wrapped across her forehead—probably not a good sign. But then, yes, yes! She was talking to one of the police officers and waving at them all as the back double doors of the ambulance were slammed shut. Whew!

"Is she gonna be okay?" Penny asked me, her face still pressed against the window.

I wasn't sure how to answer this, but with perfect timing, Mom was back in my room, cheeks flushed, smelling of antiseptic and, yep, roses!

She rubbed my and Penny's shoulders and then collapsed into a chair. "From what I could tell, and from what the paramedics said, Miss Gertie isn't seriously injured. The fall just gave her a big bonk on the head and knocked the wind out of her for a bit. Because she's older, a bump on the head can't be ignored, so they're going to run a few tests at the hospital, as a precaution. But the fact that she's now awake and talking is very promising."

"That's great news!" Dad exclaimed.

"Shouldn't you go to the hospital to take care of her?" Penny asked, almost sternly.

Mom laughed and pulled Penny onto her lap. "You'll make a great hospital supervisor one day, little one. I offered, but they've got it covered. The hospital already has plenty of nurses on shift today. I'd just be in the way."

Penny seemed satisfied with that answer; she'd already turned to watch the ambulance leave. Dad left to get Mom a cup of coffee.

"Besides," Mom told her, "I'm spending the morning with my two girls instead!"

Penny squealed happily.

I didn't respond. I had to make sure of something. Miss Gertie's Peace rosebush—had it gotten trampled? My eyes followed the path of roses up her walkway and phew—there it was, tall and blushing toward the morning sunshine.

"When will we know how she's doing?" I asked Mom.

"Hmm. Probably not for a couple of hours," she replied. "But I'll call the hospital soon to get an update on her status. I know you're worried."

I looked up, and incredibly, I noticed tears in her eyes. She sniffed. "Melody, I can't begin to tell you how impressed I am. You handled something that other people would have freaked out over, and did it all with your board." She gulped and added, "You quite possibly saved Miss Gertie's life! She might have been in serious trouble if it weren't for you!"

I half shrugged. It hadn't seemed like a big deal at the time—I was too busy being scared.

I tapped Elvira. **"I'm just glad I remembered that button!"**

"Me too. Say! How about we bake something yummy to take our minds off things?"

Penny hopped off Mom's lap with a cry of "Brownies!" and raced toward the kitchen.

I took a moment to glance out that window once more, my thoughts racing faster than Penny. What if I hadn't been sitting there? What if the dispatcher hadn't figured out what I was trying to say? What if . . . ? What if . . . ?

CHAPTER 7

The kitchen smelled like bronzed brown as Penny's treats came out of the oven. How a room smells brown, I don't know, but the air bloomed thick and chocolaty. Penny blew on the first brownie out of the pan and stuffed the whole thing into her mouth while reaching for a second one!

"Let's put the brakes on, Chocolate Monster," Mom chided. "Give the first one a chance to get to your tummy, okay?" She handed Penny a cup of milk.

Penny, mouth full, answered, "Nothin' better than too much chocolate!" Mom chuckled, but I noticed she moved the pan up to a high shelf.

She always makes a batch of vanilla ladyfingers for me

when she bakes, because she understands that me and chocolate are never gonna be best friends. I know it's extra effort, so I grinned extra hard with appreciation as she fed me a piece. She helped me sip my milk from my special cup, designed so that the person using it can't choke by gulping down too much at once. I looked at the unwieldy design and thought, *I bet I could improve on this*, and . . . my mind started doing calculations in my head. Hmm, I'd narrow the sipping part, smooth out the gulping part, and slow down the flow of the liquid. I do that all the time—invent stuff in my head that would make my life, or anybody else's life who needs it, a little easier, a little simpler.

Then I think about the fact that I'm thinking about this kind of stuff, and Mom hasn't the foggiest notion of where my mind is tiptoeing. I guess most moms have no idea what their kids are thinking, which is probably a good thing—LOL!

Suddenly the *Game of Thrones* theme song blared from Mom's phone. She loved that show so much she made it her ringtone.

"Yes, this is Mrs. Brooks," she said, answering, then paused, listened. "And uh, yes, it was my daughter who made the 911 call. And uh, no, you can't speak to her." She glanced over at me with a look that was a cross between a smirk and a frown.

Then she said in her best *Don't mess with my family* voice, "And who are you, sir?"

"I see," and "Oh, really?" came next. As I was wondering what the heck was going on, Mom said, "Oh my!" Finally, she told whoever she was talking to, "Well, I'm very proud that my daughter was able to help Miss Gilson. Thank you for your call."

She clicked off her phone, poured herself a cup of coffee, and sank into the seat next to me.

Dad, who'd just wandered in, likely lured by the smell of chocolate, asked, "Who was that on the phone?"

Mom had the strangest look on her face. "Channel 9 News!" she announced with a cough of disbelief.

I looked at her in surprise.

"What's up?" I tapped out.

"Well, *apparently* there's a lot we didn't know about Miss Gertie, and *apparently*"—now she raised an eyebrow my way—"there are a lot of other people who also think you are a hero!"

Huh? I didn't even know what to tap in response.

Dad was clearly just as confused. "I'm not following, Diane."

Mom reached for her laptop on the counter. "Hold up. Let me check something." She clicked and scrolled, then gasped. "Oh my goodness! How could I not have known?"

"What? What? What?" I tapped repeatedly.

Mom looked, well . . . almost sad. "Well, it seems our Miss Gertie, who was living across the street long before we moved here fifteen years ago, is a bit of a recluse, and also . . . famous!"

Whoa! Miss Gertie was famous?

"For . . . what?" my dad asked.

"Back in the sixties, Miss Gertie was a British film star! She was in over a dozen movies." Mom looked back at her screen. "She also starred in lots of theater productions!"

"Like *Yabba Dabba Duckie*?" Penny asked.

"No, sweetie. Yabba is a cartoon character. Miss Gertie is a real person."

"So is she still famous?" Penny asked as she picked a brownie crumb off the table and poked it into her mouth.

Mom wiped Penny's fingers with a wet wipe that she'd pulled from a half-empty package on a side table. We went through a lot of those things in this house!

"Well, fame lives with us forever, but sometimes it fades and hides."

"So she's like a *real* movie star?" Penny asked. "Did you ever talk to her?"

"I used to try," Mom explained. "I even baked her a pie once. She told me she didn't eat sweets and closed the door."

Penny looked shocked. "She didn't want *pie*?"

Mom laughed. "Yep. My famous apple deluxe! After that, I respected her privacy and never did more than share a wave in the morning, maybe a brief conversation about the weather." She frowned. "I should have been a better neighbor."

"I bet she was lonely," I tapped out, thinking again how I rarely saw anyone come to her house.

Penny suddenly looked stricken. "I bet my old Barbie dolls are lonely in the back of my closet. I never take them out because their hair is messy and I lost their clothes."

Mom and I looked at her at the same time. Penny seemed to have a deeper understanding of our conversation than I expected.

I thought about loneliness and isolation for a minute. Sometimes it *is* easier to be lonely than to try to fit in. Plus, so many of the movie stars I watch on TV are young and pretty with fancy outfits and hairstyles. And their fans, I guess, want to dress like them, modern and chic and cool. It's gotta be hard to be an older actress who used to be famous, used to wear the latest fashions, used to be a trendsetter. You look in the mirror and watch yourself get old and watch your popularity and career fade like the sunset. The thought made me give a little shiver.

But I just tapped, **"I hope she's okay."**

"I feel exactly the same way," Mom said as Dad nodded emphatically.

The *Game of Thrones* ringtone sounded again. "Hello? Yes," Mom said. And "yes" again. She paused, then said, "Could you repeat that? I'm not sure I understand."

I watched as Mom's facial expression shifted from a frown to a question mark to a look of genuine surprise. What was going on?

She whispered to us, "This time it's Channel 12 News!"

Then she said, "Please give me a moment. I'm putting the phone on speaker so that my family can hear you."

Speaker on, she asked the caller to repeat what she'd said.

"We would like to interview your daughter on the morning news!"

Wait . . . what? If I could speak, those words for sure would have shut me up!

The lady on the phone continued. "We've heard about your daughter's courage and heroism. Her swift action, under what could have been impossible circumstances, has saved the life of a British film icon."

"We're very proud of Melody," my father agreed.

"As are we. That's why we're calling. With your permission, Channel 12 News would like to interview your daughter on the air tomorrow morning. It's exactly the type of human interest story we love to highlight; something good and positive in our world. Would you be willing to bring her to our studio on Highland Avenue for our nine o'clock morning news show?"

It seemed like all the air was suddenly sucked out of the room.

My dad nodded to my mom to respond. "Uh, an interview with our daughter might be . . ." She paused, then added carefully, "A bit complicated. She uses a wheelchair."

"Everything in our studio is on the same floor," the caller said quickly, already anticipating what my parents were thinking. "We are one hundred percent accessible. We'd be honored to meet Melody and, well, all of you. Could you be here around eight o'clock?"

I was starting to freak out. Me? On the news? For real?!

As if this happened every day, Mom nodded to Dad, Dad nodded to Mom, then Mom cooed, "Of course! We'd be delighted. Thank you! We'll see you in the morning!"

She hung up. We all blinked at each other, until—I couldn't believe it—my sensible, serious, careful mother screeched, "We're gonna be on TV!"

CHAPTER 8

Okay, so Mom was on a mission. She had less than twenty-four hours to get her family ready for a television appearance. I figured we'd be on the air for, at the most, five minutes, but Mom acted like she was preparing for battle. Dad stayed out of her way, but he winked at me and Penny from time to time.

In Penny's room, Mom laid out two outfits for her—a blue dress and a red dress—and told her to choose one.

Penny wailed, "But I wanna wear my yabba-yellow jeans!"

Yabba-yellow jeans, by the way, are what the characters wear on the *Yabba Dabba Duckie* show.

Mom told her, in a voice she rarely used for Penny, "Blue dress or red dress. Pick one!"

Penny's eyes widened, but she wisely pointed to the red dress. She didn't even glance at the yellow jeans.

"I'm sorry, sweetie," Mom told her a moment later. "I didn't mean to yell. You'll look lovely in red when we go on television."

"How we gonna get inside the TV?" Penny asked.

It occurred to me that my sister had no idea how television programs worked. She just clicked the remote or tapped her tablet and her shows magically appeared. But even I wasn't even completely sure of the technological process of broadcasting a television show.

Mom explained, "In the morning, we are going to drive downtown to a television studio. Inside, there are cameras and lights and people who tell us the news—that's information about important things that are happening in our world. And for now, your sister has become part of that news."

"So Dee-Dee is important?"

"Absolutely!" Mom said. "And so are you. And tomorrow all of us are going to be on the morning newscast!"

Zillions of tiny details must be zooming through Mom's brain at that moment—getting a family like ours ready for television was probably a little staggering.

"Will we get to see *Yabba Dabba Duckie*?" Penny asked hopefully. "He lives inside the TV."

"Probably not, sweetie. Yabba will probably be off on another adventure."

Penny's face showed a flash of disappointment, but her thoughts had already bounced to another question.

"Uh, do the TV people know how to talk to Melody? Sometimes strangers don't know about the hurricane stuck inside her head."

Gotta say, I was amazed at the depth of this kid sometimes.

"You are the best little sister in the world, my Penny Princess," Mom told her. "We'll make absolute sure that Melody's voice is heard loud and clear!"

Satisfied, Penny scooted into the closet and grabbed a couple of naked Barbies, then searched in a pile for outfits for them. Holding one scraggly-haired doll in each hand, she whispered to them, "You can't be inside the TV with us 'cause you're naked. Too bad I lost your princess dresses."

I snort-laughed.

Mom now turned to me. "You're the reason for this adventure, Melody. What would you like to wear?"

I hardly ever wear dresses. They're pretty, but the shorter ones don't cover my knobby knees, and the longer ones sometimes get caught in the spokes of my wheelchair. But I had a brand-new dark-blue-and-turquoise dress that Mrs. V had given me when I got back from camp. So I tapped out, **"New one."**

Mom nodded in agreement. "The one V gave you? Perfect. She'll be so pleased!"

Just then the doorbell rang. Penny, seeing Mrs. V from the window, ran to open the door. Our neighbor swooshed into the living room. I say swooshed because Mrs. V never just walked anywhere. She moved with purpose and flair at all times, and always wore a colorful outfit that seemed to flow along with her. Today's was purple and gold.

"Guess what, Mrs. V!" Penny waved her naked Barbies in the air. "I'm gonna be on TV tomorrow!"

"Well, that's exciting news." Mrs. V squatted down to Penny's eye level. "Are you going to be on television by yourself?"

"No, silly. Mom and Dad and Dee-Dee will be there too! But probably not Yabba Dabba Duckie," she added somberly. "And not the naked Barbies."

"Thank goodness for that!" Mrs. V said as Mom and I laughed. "Your mom told me what happened this morning, and I could hardly be more impressed by what you did for Miss Gertie," she said to me, coming over.

I tapped out, **"I just called 911—anybody could have done that."**

Seriously, all this attention was making me a little self-conscious.

"Yes, that's true." Mrs. V crossed her arms. "But nobody else did. And without you, there's no telling how long Miss Gertie might have lain there. You, Melody Brooks, are a hero!"

People kept calling me a hero, but I never thought about it that way. Saved her life? Those are words that are said in movies. Gritty action performed by soldiers with guns on the battlefield; superhero folk in colorful capes who fly and swoop and save a city from a monster. Clearly, I've watched too much TV. Also clear—none of those descriptions fit me. I was just a girl who made a phone call.

"I called the hospital a little while ago and talked to my supervisor, who knows all," Mom told us all. "Miss Gertie will probably be released tomorrow. But for now, they are treating her like the movie star that she is!"

Hearing that Miss Gertie was going to be okay made me feel a little less gurgly in my stomach, and gave me an idea.

So I tapped, **"Would it be okay if we visited Miss Gertie at the hospital this afternoon?"**

Truth? Hospitals kinda freak me out a little, but Miss Gertie deserved to know someone cared about her.

Mom immediately nodded. "That's really thoughtful of you!"

Mrs. V looked to my mother. "Don't you work a late shift tonight, Diane? And you've got the big television thing tomorrow. Why don't you let me take the girls to see Miss Gertie? Take some time for yourself this afternoon."

I could see the relief and thanks on Mom's face. She didn't get many kid-free afternoons.

"Bless you, V," she said. "I'd really appreciate that."

"That's what friends are for." Mrs. V sorta sang her answer—she's a trip.

After lunch of buttered noodles and peanut butter on a spoon (for me) and peanut butter and jelly on raisin bread (for Penny), Mom strapped Penny into the car seat in Mrs. V's car. Then she lifted me into a specially-made-for-me, much larger car seat. Mrs. V had duplicates of everything we needed. I'd never really thought about it much, but she was like Mom's second right hand. She was always there when we needed her. Mom loaded my chair, waved goodbye, and headed back to the house, Butterscotch at her heels.

At the hospital, even Penny's usual exuberance was dialed back a notch. She looked around, eyes wide with wonder at the calm but busy lobby, full of folks sitting, waiting, or hustling to their destinations in other parts of the hospital.

What was cool was that no one, literally nobody, looked at me! For once I fit into a crowd! LOL. Mrs. V asked about Miss Gertie at the reception desk.

"Room 507, ma'am," a nurse said, then turned quickly to the next person in line.

The first thing I saw on the fifth floor was a circular area filled with desks and monitors and beeping equipment, and maybe ten or twelve nurses or doctors. Some were on computers, some were wheeling trays of food, and some were hurrying from one area to another. It was the most organized chaos I'd ever seen.

Mrs. V approached a large man in blue scrubs and purple Crocs. He was looking down at a tablet, his brow furrowed in concentration.

She cleared her throat. "Excuse me, sir. We are looking for room 507. Can you point us in that direction?"

The guy looked up with a grin. "You're here to see Miss Gertie? What a wonderful lady! Her room is the sixth one on the left." He nodded in that direction. "Glad she's got some visitors!"

Mrs. V thanked him. Each room we passed had a tag outside it, stating the patient's name in bold letters. The halls themselves were decorated with murals of flowers and birds, popping with color. It was like the hospital was trying really hard to make a sometimes scary, sometimes sad place as cheerful as possible. I appreciated that.

See, I've had lots of hospital visits over the years, and dozens and dozens of doctor appointments. I've been tested and probed and measured. I've had doctors scratch their heads in confusion when they finally figured out that even though my body shows up like a plate of wet spaghetti, my mind is a ten-course meal!

But for real, seems to me the people who work in hospitals are doing their best to make what is sometimes a bad situation a little bit better, and it seems like they genuinely care about their patients. I should know—I've been there, done that, been that patient, soooo many times.

When we got to room 507, the name GERTRUDE GILSON was printed in red marker outside her door. I'd never even thought about her last name before.

We paused. Should we knock?

We didn't have time to decide because the door opened with a whoosh and a woman in green scrubs hurried out. We rolled in on her energy. In fact, I felt suddenly nervous, speechless.

Miss Gertie, dressed in a pale blue hospital gown, lay against a pillow. Her eyes were closed. An IV tube ran into her arm, while soft beeping noises came from a machine that I guess did . . . something? I had no idea. So much for TV shows.

Penny grabbed Mrs. V's arm with one hand and mine with her other. "Should we wake her up?" she whispered.

"I'm not asleep." We all jumped!

Miss Gertie looked over at us and said with a faint British accent, "I was just resting my eyes." She smiled.

I don't think I'd ever seen her smile before . . . well, maybe when she was talking to her roses. But never at the mail carrier or the electric-meter-checking person who stopped by our houses from time to time.

"My big sister saw you fall down!" Penny blurted out.

Now Miss Gertie turned to me.

"And she called the polices and the amboolance and everybody!" Penny informed her, a bit of sass in her voice.

"So that was you!" Miss Gertie exclaimed. "Then I owe you a tremendous thanks. What's your name?"

Penny started to answer, but I gave her the side-eye and tapped my board.

"I'm Melody. And that's Penny, my sister."

Miss Gertie didn't seem the least bit surprised that I answered through a machine.

"Well, Melody, I'm very glad you made that call." She gave a sweet, bubbly laugh. "I don't remember much except waking up to a very handsome paramedic trying to resuscitate me."

Seeing her laugh was a little weird. I'd always thought she was kinda grumpy. I mean, she'd wave at me, but she never really talked to anyone. And now I felt bad. It turned out she was just a nice old lady.

So I laughed as well.

"You gonna be okay?" Penny asked.

"Yes, dear. I think I shall!" She scooched up a little on her pillow, gently touched the bandage on her forehead.

"That's wonderful to hear," Mrs. V said. "And we've waved to each other, but I'm Violet—I live kitty-corner across the street from you. I'll be sure to water your roses and check your mail and such for as long as you need, ma'am."

"I appreciate that." Miss Gertie smoothed out her sheet. "And please don't call me 'ma'am.' I'm Gertie to my friends, and I've decided that you are now my friends!"

Unexpectedly, this caused Penny to frown. "But you don't like pie."

Miss Gertie looked surprised. "Pie? But I love pie!" she said finally. "Blueberry is my favorite."

Penny's face went stern. "Mommy made you a pie a long time ago," she muttered, a hint of accusation in her voice. "But you told her you didn't like pie."

Miss Gertie paused, then after a moment answered, "I'm sorry, sweet girl. Sometimes when sorrow takes over, kindness can hide from you."

I wasn't sure if Penny understood, but I glanced at Mrs. V and we nodded at each other.

Miss Gertie continued. "Years and years ago, I had a career I loved, and a husband I loved even more. We traveled the world together, appearing in films and performing live on stage. We lived in a lovely flat in London that was walking distance to the Thames River and all the theaters you'd ever want to see. And oh, so many museums!"

"Which ones?" I tapped, curious.

"The British Museum, for one. And the Victoria and Albert Museum! From royal crowns to the world's first Christmas card, to an eight-foot-wide petticoat, the V&A could entrance me for days."

I giggled, picturing myself in an eight-foot petticoat.

Miss Gertie, clearly enjoying these memories of her hometown, continued. "The Natural History Museum has over a million fossil specimens. Plus, there's the Science Museum—it's got part of a real Boeing 747 in there somewhere!"

I was thinking, *Those must be awesome.*

Miss Gertie gave a soft sigh, a distant look in her eyes. "I'd love to see my London again."

"Do you have family there?" Mrs. V asked.

"Yes, I do." But she said no more.

Just as I was thinking maybe it was time to go, Penny piped up with, "Did you ever see dinosaurs?"

And just like that, Miss Gertie was laughing again.

"No, sweetie. No dinosaurs, but I do remember black-and-white televisions and telephones that you had to dial—well before cellular phones! You called your friends on a big black phone that hung on your kitchen wall."

"But only if your mother let you!" Mrs. V added wryly.

Miss Gertie's eyes lit up. "The first cell phones were those big fat Motorolas! The size of a shoe!"

"We handwrote letters to friends, and mailed them with a stamp!"

"Why didn't you just use ZibberZabber?" Penny asked.

"Social media hadn't been invented yet!" Mrs. V and Miss Gertie said nearly in unison.

My brain was scrambling, trying to imagine this world they were describing.

They kept going:

"If you wanted to find some information, you had to look it up in an encyclopedia," Miss Gertie continued.

It must have taken forever to find out anything!

"Cameras contained an actual roll of film inside!" Miss Gertie said.

"And we had to take them to the drugstore and wait

a week for the film to get developed!" Mrs. V finished.

Miss Gertie laughed so hard she began to cough.

I made a grunt and pointed toward the pitcher of water on the bedside tray. Mrs. V nodded, poured some water into a paper cup, and held it up to Miss Gertie's lips. She took a grateful sip, then started up again.

"Speaking of roll, we watched rock and roll get born!"

"Which we mostly listened to on radios."

"Elvis Presley!"

"The Beatles!"

"Little Richard!"

"Doris Day!"

"Etta James!"

Whoa, this was old-school for sure. So cool.

It was like Miss Gertie and Mrs. V were playing a verbal volleyball game.

"Most kids played outside every day with their friends," Mrs. V said.

"And we rode our bikes miles away from home."

That caught my attention. It must have been really hard for kids like me back when Miss Gertie was a kid.

"Google Maps didn't exist. We used giant, fold-out paper maps that were free at the gas station."

Paper maps? How the heck would you drive and look at a big old map at the same time?

Miss Gertie looked thoughtful for a moment. "My

mother always wore a hat, shined leather shoes, and white gloves—even to the grocery store!"

"No jeans?" I tapped.

She shook her head. "Heavens no! Mother would have been horrified!" Cheeks pink, she asked for another sip of water. "This has been great fun. I honestly did not expect many visitors. When one is my age, one has very few friends left."

"You got me!" Penny exclaimed, her curls bouncing. "And Dee-Dee and Mrs. V too!"

Miss Gertie clasped her hands. "I do, indeed."

"And Dee-Dee is gonna be on TV tomorrow!" Penny announced with pride.

"As she should be." Miss Gertie reached for my hand, surprising me. Most people are scared to do that. Her hand was soft, like a small bird.

"I'm very thankful for what you did, Melody. Who knows what might have happened. . . ." Then she whispered to Penny, "And if the doctor gives the okay, I'm going to be joining you on TV tomorrow."

She was? Me . . . and a movie star? What universe was this? Before I could react, Mrs. V said we really ought to be heading home.

"I hope we haven't exhausted you with our little visit," she said, apology in her voice.

Miss Gertie protested immediately. "No, no, no! I'm

chuffed to have company. I hadn't realized how . . . lonely I've gotten."

"Chuffed?" asked Penny.

"Oh, we say that in England when we mean 'very happy.' It's a fun word, isn't it?" Miss Gertie explained. Penny nodded enthusiastically, murmuring "chuffed chuffed chuffed."

A nurse stepped into the room, gave us a smile, and began checking the gauges and tubes and monitors by Miss Gertie's bed.

"Well," Mrs. V said into the silence, "we've taken up enough of Miss Gertie's time." She looked pointedly at me and Penny.

"Can we come back?" Penny asked.

"Oh, Miss Gertie will be released tomorrow, honey."

I tapped on my board, **"May I visit you when you get home, Miss Gertie?"**

"I'd like that very much, Melody."

She waved as we turned to leave the room. Somehow I had made a friend of a zillion-year-old lady. I sure didn't expect that when I woke up this morning.

"And like I said, don't worry for one moment about your Tropicanas—I'll keep an eye on them until you're fit as a fiddle," Mrs. V assured her.

"I appreciate that," Miss Gertie replied. "As long as it doesn't take time away from your blue jays."

"You know about them?" Mrs. V asked.

"The whole neighborhood knows about those squawking birds. They make themselves heard!" Miss Gertie laughed. "Just because I keep to myself doesn't mean I don't know what's going on."

CHAPTER 9

My brain was sizzling when I got home. I was obsessed with England! First I watched a documentary about Queen Elizabeth. The processionals, the precision of the soldiers, the parades and pageantry. Ha! I'm using a million words that start with the letter *P*! Me and words— we've got it going on, even if it's mostly in my head!

I couldn't get enough of it all. And whoa—the bagpipes! They sounded ancient and futuristic, like they might be ordinary music on the planet Mars. I could listen to them all day! I pumped up the volume. Dad looked into my room as if to say, *What the heck?* Then he just shook his head and left.

I read about King Arthur and *Beowulf* and Chaucer. I then found an old movie about King Arthur and the Knights of the Round Table and watched that next. Who knew English history was so fascinating? Well, now I did. Wars were won with gleaming magical swords. Knights in armor fought on horseback—and the horses wore armor too! And there were dozens of kings and queens, all of whom lived in fine castles and had juicy stories to be discovered. I couldn't believe Miss Gertie grew up there!

After dinner, I looked up films and plays that she had been in. Yowzer! There were lots. *Love's Last Laugh. Heavenly Haven. MacBeth. King Lear. Piccadilly Predicament.* I rolled into the living room and watched the one about the clouds. It was soooo good. She played the part of a lonely girl who had fallen in love with a farmer's son. She was really good! And it was amazing to see her so young. She had the type of smile that made *you* want to smile!

I almost forgot about our visit to the TV station tomorrow. Almost.

Until Mom came in, a strange look on her face.

"What's wrong?" I asked. **"Why aren't you at the hospital?"**

"Oh, nothing's wrong. They were overstaffed so I got to leave early. But I've got something incredible to show you!" Mom perched next to me on the sofa. "So, I was just online, checking something. . . ." She paused. "And

Melody, you are trending *number one* on ZibberZabber."

I gasped. Me?? ZibberZabber is the most popular social media site in the country, maybe even the world. Famous people use it. All the kids at school use it. Everybody who is anybody uses it. So no way am I, me, a nobody, trending. No way.

"News of you saving Miss Gertie's life is the biggest story of the day. You have thousands of new followers!" She looked from me, to the phone, then to me, then the phone—as if she couldn't believe it.

I blinked, trying to process this information.

Mom gave me more to take in by adding, "The television station has called several times, making sure you will be there tomorrow. Two other stations want to interview you as well!"

"What did you tell them?" I tapped, suddenly panicky.

"I told them that Channel 12 had the exclusive, and they would just have to watch you there! I also told Channel 12 what was going on, and they were *very* pleased that I had done that."

The *Game of Thrones* theme song rang out, and Mom was on the phone again.

I wheeled myself to my room, opened ZibberZabber on Elvira, and OMG—there I was! Plain old ordinary, can't-walk, can't-talk Melody was all over the place. There were pictures of me from camp (where did they get those?), horrible school photos (that I always look extra goofy in), and even baby pictures that Mom had posted online back when I was little.

I jabbed the off button with my thumb, breathing hard, feeling oddly upset. Nobody asked me if I wanted to be all over the internet. Or having old pictures of me shown everywhere. Loads of people do nice things every day. So why me? Because I'm what they call "disabled"? Because a kid like me isn't expected to be able to do something like this?

Mom came into my room a few minutes later. I tried to wipe my face so she couldn't see I'd been crying. My arms wouldn't cooperate, of course. Mom sat down in the rocking chair and waited.

When the tears kept rolling, my eyes not cooperating either, Mom finally said, "We can cancel the TV interview. All this will go away in no time."

I shook my head. My legs kicked.

"I just want you to think about something." She hesitated, waiting for me to nod okay, so I did.

"Being famous, even for a minute, can be a gift, and can offer the power to implement positive change in the world."

Huh. I hadn't considered that.

My legs stopped kicking. I lifted my head. I sniffed as Mom wiped my nose with a tissue.

Okaaay. **"That's kinda deep,"** I tapped. Who knew my mother was so profound?

She laughed. "I can't take credit for it. I'd heard a quote once, from Sean Lennon, the son of one of the Beatles, and that was the gist of it."

So I tapped out, **"Before I change my mind, let's do it. How many times does a kid like me get a chance like this?"**

"Exactly!" Mom took my bendy-twisty hand in hers and shook it like we were making a deal.

CHAPTER 10

I woke up the next morning buzzing, not sure if I was excited or terrified. Probably a little of both. Mom came in all full of energy. "Are you ready to rumble?" She loved that phrase—an oldie from back in the day to introduce professional boxing matches on television. Why two people would want to get beat up on TV was beyond me, but here I was, about to do almost the same thing!

Okay, so nobody was going to hit me, but I've seen interviews before, and sometimes the interviewer drops a sucker-punch question to the person sitting on the stage. It makes for good TV, but I bet the person who gets asked the embarrassing question feels pretty bad. I hoped I didn't get sucker punched today.

We managed to get me dressed without much issue. As Mom rolled me past the mirror, I was kinda surprised— I looked pretty good. And Dad said I looked great, so I guess I need to wear more blue!

Penny kept asking if there was even a teeny-tiny chance of meeting Yabba Dabba Duckie. Dad checked his watch constantly while he fed me, after wrapping two towels around my neck—no spills were gonna mess up this day!

Mom, well, she was on fire. She made Dad change his tie. Twice. He grumbled—twice. But the ones he had picked out first were pretty ugly, I had to admit.

Mom finally changed from her jeans into a silky burgundy dress, which was decorated with golden buttons and a shiny belt, and matching high heels I'd never seen before, which made her three inches taller. She must keep those in the "hardly ever used" section of her closet.

Plus, she was wearing makeup—eyeliner and lipstick and mascara! I hardly ever saw my mother all dressed up. She was either in blue scrubs, heading to work, or in jeans or comfy sweats at home. But this morning she looked runway ready.

Dad noticed too. He grabbed her waist, spun her

around like they were ballroom dancers, then kissed her cheek. They hugged, then grinned at me and Penny.

"You look like a movie star!" Penny whispered.

Mom beamed. "My whole family does this morning. Let's get to this studio while we've got it all together. We look awesome!"

Then she put Butterscotch in a back bedroom so that not even one random speck of golden retriever fluff would mess up our clothes.

Finally, after a last-minute run to the bathroom for Penny, we hurried to the car. It took about fifteen minutes to load up—my electric wheelchair, Penny's bag of Barbies—some of them, yep, still naked—and Mom's bag of emergency items. She'd stuffed in photos of me as a baby (after making sure I was cool with it), just-in-case wet wipes, as well as juice boxes and fruit snacks for Penny, and a couple of pudding cups.

I figured the drive, in morning traffic, would take about a half hour, but Dad wanted to leave way early, just in case, because "rush hour can snarl you up forever!" And when we hit one mini traffic snarl, he exclaimed almost happily, "See, it's a good thing we left early!" But we got there with no hiccups.

After the unloading scramble, and Dad having to go back for the bag of Barbies, I rolled myself up the wide ramp to the front door of Channel 12. Points for the studio—instead of having both steps and a ramp, they had a slightly inclined walkway, which doubled as a ramp for anyone who needed it. Brilliant!

The glass entry door opened automatically, as if it were expecting us, and we found ourselves in a living-room-looking lobby area. A massive screen was showing a live traffic update—a woman dressed in purple, pointing to the map of our area, chatted about a single construction delay. She predicted a day of sun-smooth travel. That was because she couldn't see the storm of nerves brewing inside me.

When Dad gave the receptionist our names, the man's smile went from ear to ear.

"Welcome, Brooks family!" he cried out. "There's no need for you to wait here in the lobby. Take a left, and the studio will be just ahead. Miss Gilson is already here. We picked her up in a limo."

A limo? Wowzer!

Mom gave us one last once-over to make sure there were no unruly bits of clothing, brushed a dog hair off Dad's jacket, added a barrette to Penny's hair, and wiped my face in case I'd drooled. She was in Supersonic Mom Mode.

When we at last met with her approval, we headed down the hall, and . . . wow! Suddenly we were in a

TV studio! It was roomy—with about ten humongous cameras and other complicated-looking equipment and massive lights everywhere.

And ooh, there was Leonardo Fontana, one of the top newscasters! He was giving a report about a war in Indonesia. He read from a teleprompter, so he didn't have to look down at notes. Aha! I'm not the only one who uses a machine to sound intelligent!

Mr. Fontana, who seemed even more charming in person than on the screen—just saying—then switched effortlessly to the next subject. "Here in town, the new housing construction project in Lincoln Heights is well underway. Dozens of new homes will be available in just a few months. For more information, please call Realtors Elaine Harris or Darlene Hampton at the number on your screen. And now for your local weather update. How's it looking out there today, Wally?"

The screen then displayed a map of the city, and the cameras shifted to the guy who was simply called Wally Weather. He must have had a real name, but I'd never heard it. We watched him all the time, because it's tricky for me to go out in bad weather. My wheelchair doesn't like it!

I looked around:

The twisted black cables at my feet.

Television cameras, the size of televisions, everywhere!

The surge of energy as some of those cameras were being moved to the interview area.

I wondered if any of the kids from school or camp would see this. I kinda hoped so.

While Wally was doing his weather thing, also reading from a teleprompter, a lady with an earphone in one ear and a clipboard in one hand rushed over to us. "I'm Chantal," she whispered. "Let me get you set up with mics, Brooks family."

She deftly snapped a microphone onto Dad's tie, onto the neck of Mom's dress, and even on Penny's. She then squatted down, so she and I would be at eye level. "I've got you covered, Melody. I've done some research to make sure everything would go smoothly for you today." Even her smile was calming. "We're going to connect a microphone to the speaker on your board. So you can tap your answers out just like you're used to. You and Miss Gilson are going to be interviewed by one of our best journalists, Ron Dodson. He's terrific."

I'd watched the Dodson and Fontana morning show a bunch of times. Mr. Dodson loved to laugh, but he asked hard questions. Mr. Fontana picked up where Mr. Dodson left off. Their reporting was synched, quick, and always got your attention.

I gulped. It only took a minute to get me miked up. A commercial about deodorant for stinky feet was playing.

I seriously felt like I was on another planet. The massive lights above us were so bright they made me blink. I wonder where they bought light bulbs that big!

Penny whispered, "I can't believe I'm inside the TV for real!"

I felt the same way.

Then I saw Miss Gertie. She looked . . . glamorous! She had on a silvery-gray silk dress, a double strand of pearls, black patent-leather boots—yes, boots—and long white gloves, the kind I've seen on old ballroom dancing shows. Her *pièce de résistance* (yeah, I've been paying attention to my French lessons) was a peacock-blue hat with two simple feathers—one silver-gray, one deep navy. The hat deftly covered a small white bandage that was all that remained of her earlier one. Instead of looking weak and wan like she had in the hospital, her cheeks were blushed, her back was straight, her eyes were shining. She waved us over.

"Hi," I tapped shyly when we reached her.

"It's lovely to see you again, Melody." Her voice was clear and strong, as if yesterday had never happened.

"Are you all better now?" Penny asked.

"Well, Miss Penny, they booted me out of the hospital, so I guess I'm fine!" She patted my sister's hand.

We didn't have time to say anything more because someone in a headset yelled out, "Two minutes!"

A staff member guided Miss Gertie over to the interview area and helped her sit down. A technician slipped a tiny microphone onto the collar of her dress.

Ron Dodson took a seat in the interviewer's chair, which looked smaller in real life, as Mr. Fontana perched in the chair beside him. They scanned their notes.

Mr. Dodson checked the camera angles, then called out cheerily, "Come on over, Melody! Bring your family. You and Miss Gilson are the celebrities of the morning!"

Mom rolled me over to what the technicians were calling "center stage," right beside Miss Gertie, then she and Dad stood nervously behind me. Penny clung to the armrest of my wheelchair. I clung to the hope that I wouldn't throw up.

Suddenly, on the monitor directly in front of me, and somehow also on each side, was my face—up close and personal. Yikes! I looked . . . I looked, uh, like myself, but weird. What would the people watching this think of me? Would they think I was funny-looking or ugly, or goofy? I hoped I wouldn't drool. What if my arms decided to do their arm dance? OMG! What if I kicked over a camera? Kicking over a camera was exactly what my legs might decide to do! Just thinking that made one leg swing out a little.

Dad grabbed my hand and, giving it a squeeze, whispered, "You are the sun and the moon and the stars right now, Melody. It won't last long, so relax and enjoy this moment."

Right. Right. Right. It was a *moment.* I could do a moment! So I did.

A blast of some sort of trumpet sounded as it did every show, and now it was blasting for me and Miss Gertie. I couldn't believe we were here!!!

"Good morning, news fans! I'm Ron Dodson, and today we have a young heroine and the 'lost treasure' she discovered and saved!"

That was kinda overboard on the hype, but I smiled as best I could, and managed a wobbly wave.

Mr. Dodson gave a quick recap of what had happened yesterday morning—wow, could he make things sound ten times more exciting than they were!—then leaned forward, hands on his knees, and finished with, "And the lost treasure Melody saved is Miss Gertrude Gilson, star of the award-winning film *Heavenly Haven* among many others, as well as leading lady in many Shakespearean plays, including *Twelfth Night, The Tempest,* and *Romeo and Juliet.*"

Miss Gertie tipped her head elegantly toward the camera.

"So, Miss Gilson, it turns out that you've been living quietly right here in our town, and few of us were aware. How does it feel to be back under the studio lights?"

Miss Gertie ran a finger along her strand of pearls. "Well, I've been fortunate enough to have had more than my fair share of screen time. In all honesty, I haven't felt the pull of the stage or screen for decades now. But being here has awakened beautiful memories of when I was acting under lights like these." She paused. "I've become a bit of a recluse, you see. After my beloved Jasper passed away, I lost the desire to perform."

She took a deep breath. "But the *reason* I'm here now is what's so special to me. Despite working to stay out of the spotlight, I managed to find my way back due to an amazing young lady." Miss Gertie swung her arms out almost ballerina-like. "Melody here saved my life in ways she probably cannot imagine."

The two reporters cheesed for the camera.

I could hardly smile back, my brain too busy processing what she'd said.

Mr. Dodson, nodding so hard he looked like a bobble-head doll, swiftly turned toward me.

"So . . . Melody, what does it feel like to be a hero at the age of twelve? You single-handedly saved the life of another human being by calling 911 and alerting the authorities. And all without being able to speak yourself. Your presence of mind was truly impressive."

I knew I had to answer, and I knew they didn't want to hear what my brain was insisting: that I was not a hero! Anybody would have done the same. It felt weird to claim I was!

So I began to tap as quickly as I could and let Elvira speak for me: **"I'm just glad Miss Gertie is okay and I've made a new friend."**

Mr. Fontana had a kind of proud papa look on his face. "The 911 dispatcher has nothing but praise for you and your quick thinking in a dire situation. He said, and I quote, that it makes his job worthwhile when he sees the positive impact that one human being can have on another."

I squirmed, my left leg kicking out.

Mr. Dodson's next question was about ZibberZabber. "What does it feel like to be trending number one on the most popular social media site in the world?"

"I simply do not have the words to tell you!" I tapped. I smirked, then added, **"I don't have the words to say much of anything!"** Then I broke into giggles.

After a tiny pause, Ron Dodson laughed as well, first slowly, then with hearty guffaws. Mr. Fontana joined him.

The tension was broken; I finally relaxed.

Mr. Fontana, positively beaming, leaned toward Miss Gertie next. I saw on the monitor how the camera focused in on her face, luminescent under the studio's lighting. Her eyes were as bright and shining as they'd been in *Heavenly Haven.* Her wrinkles somehow made her even more grand—kinda queenlike.

"Might you now consider a return to acting?" he asked cajolingly. "I'm sure there are theaters and studios that would love to have you back, especially now, when there are more and more roles for seasoned actresses."

Miss Gertie waved her hand as if to brush the idea away. "You are kind, Leo, but I no longer have a desire to be in the limelight. I just want to take care of my roses and . . . maybe take more time to get to know my neighbors, which I didn't do much of before all this, I'm embarrassed to say."

"Well, you've enchanted audiences for decades—and you've earned your roses," Mr. Fontana agreed.

Mr. Dodson chimed in. "If you had one wish, Miss Gilson, what would that be?"

"Well . . ." Her voice trailed off. The studio went silent. I noticed a faraway look in her eye. "Because of Melody, I've tiptoed into the greater world once more. And I actually did have one thought. . . ."

Mr. Dodson leaned in closer, eyebrows raised encouragingly. "Yes?"

"Well, while I'm rather useless on the internet, I've been looking about on airline websites. They are impossibly complicated! But it'd be grand to visit my family—my dear husband's relatives, and a few of my own. It's been far too many years."

"Do they live here in the States?" Mr. Fontana asked.

"Oh, no! Most live in London or thereabouts."

"Ah, England!" Mr. Dodson exclaimed.

"Yes. Some cousins, two nieces and nephews, and several great-nieces and great-nephews, some I've never met!" She looked down at her hands, the skin thin and stretched-looking. Was she trembling?

I've been in the same situation—having thoughts stuck way down in my guts. I wanted to pat her hand, but knowing me, my hand would fling up and knock off her cute little hat.

Then a bubble of happy rose in me. Miss Gertie wasn't entirely alone!

"Have you ever been to London, Melody?" Mr. Dodson startled me by asking.

I tapped **"NO"** real quick. Besides summer camp, my trips have been confined to the grocery store, school, Target (my happy place!), and a couple of times, the zoo.

Mr. Dodson nodded to Mr. Fontana, then announced, "Folks, we're going to take a quick commercial break. But we'll be right back with our heroine in a wheelchair, and our movie star, who's been hiding in plain sight for years!"

The cameras and the bright lights blinked off, and I exhaled. Miss Gertie sank back into her chair, looking tired. Still, she caught my eye. "You're doing marvelously, young lady. I expected nothing less."

I grinned and gave a crooked wave.

Mom rushed over to wipe my mouth and straighten my clothes. She leaned in close. "You are the bomb, Melody!"

I managed not to roll my eyes. That phrase was so fifty years ago! Before I had a chance to tell her that, the stage lights blinked back on, and Mom slipped back behind me. Mr. Fontana had smoothed his hair, and . . . was that a different tie he was wearing? He was famous for his ties—all totally extra. He'd changed from a red one with roses on it, to a pale blue one with some kind of bird on it. Was that a blue jay? Whoa! This guy had to be psychic.

And suddenly we were live again.

Mr. Fontana began. "Welcome back, ladies and gentlemen. If you are just tuning in, we are here today with Miss Melody Brooks, a twelve-year-old with extraordinary skills. You may remember hearing about her in the news a year ago; she was a key member of the nationally recognized Whiz Kids quiz team. Melody most recently saved the life of Miss Gertrude Gilson, a woman who's been living under the radar next door to Melody, and whose fame as an actress is also extraordinary. Also a rose connoisseur, we are grateful to have Miss Gilson here with us today." He paused dramatically, edging forward on his seat. He and Mr. Dodson beamed at each other. Then he announced, "Once each year we here at Channel 12 give out what we call our Humanitarian Hallelujah!"

I thought it sounded kinda cheesy, so for once it was a good thing I couldn't talk!

Then he asked me, "Have you ever heard of I.D.E.A.? It stands for 'Innovation, Discovery, Energy, and Application.'"

I scrunched my forehead, trying to figure out why he was asking this.

"Well, I.D.E.A. is an organization that was first formed about twenty years ago by a young woman in England. The most gifted and visionary young people on the planet come together once a year to exchange ideas and strategize solutions to the problems of the world. Young mathematicians, artists, scientists, designers, creators, all sorts of thinkers!"

Cool, but what did this have to do with me?

Mr. Fontana went on. "My staff has done some checking, and it seems that I.D.E.A. is having their next symposium in two weeks"—now he raised his eyebrows so high they nearly met his hairline—"in London, England!"

Miss Gertie pressed a gloved hand against her chest. I shot a glance toward Mom.

Mr. Dodson, with delight in his voice, took the lead. "As a reward for her bravery and swift thinking . . . for this year's Humanitarian Hallelujah, we would like to send Melody Brooks, along with an adult companion, to London, to attend this year's I.D.E.A. symposium! We think she would be an excellent delegate and a powerful contributor." Applause immediately broke out.

What? What? What? London?? A camera operator rolled his machine even closer to my face. I looked every bit as surprised and confused as I felt.

"In addition," Mr. Dodson continued, "if she will accept it, we here at Channel 12 would like to send Miss Gilson to London as well, so that she can visit her family."

Miss Gertie now pressed her gloved hands against her cheeks. Her mouth was a perfect O of delight.

My own hands started doing their flappy dance of happiness. The applause was even louder!

Could this be real? Were my ears working right?

Swelling music came from speakers somewhere— "Chariots of Fire," I think. Confetti, somehow, was falling from the ceiling. Did they always keep confetti in the rafters? Everyone in the studio was cheering.

As the confetti snowed down, I sat there covered with papery white flakes. Miss Gertie kept opening her mouth as if to say something, then closing it again.

When everyone finally settled down, Mr. Dodson announced his next segment.

"Our next guest is an author who wrote the book *The Zen Joy of House Cleaning*. We might need her wisdom for this mess we just made!" He chuckled, then turned to me and Miss Gertie. "Thank you both for joining us this morning. The station will be in touch with you about the details."

I was glad we weren't getting details now, because my mind had officially exploded.

London? Me?

CHAPTER 11

After about a zillion conversations with my parents about them being comfortable with me doing this, my biggest question was still, what could Melody Brooks offer to an important organization like I.D.E.A.? Of course I went into full research mode when we got home. People like Malala Yousafzai and Greta Thunberg had given presentations there! Let's just say I was big-time intimidated.

The next day, the travel coordinator from Channel 12 called. Mom put her phone on speaker so I could listen.

"Hey there, Brooks family. My name is Marisol, and I've been given the awesome task of helping plan Melody's weeklong trip to London."

Mom's first words were, "Well, sending my daughter to another country is more than a little frightening."

"I completely understand." Marisol's voice was a blend of soothing and encouraging. "My job is to ease your fears and eliminate any difficulties."

"Thank you. I very much appreciate that." Mom took a deep breath, then said, "The first thing to know is that Melody will need a full-time aide."

I made a silly face and pretended to start falling out of my chair. Mom make-believe swatted at me.

"Absolutely!" Marisol said assuredly. "It's why the trip is for two. Great minds! Have you already thought of who else might like a free trip to England?" Her laugh was tinkly and pleasant. "You, perhaps, or Melody's father?"

"Oh, I wish I could join her," Mom said, "but I can't get away from my job at the hospital—I'm the trainer for the new nursing staff, and her father has just been appointed assistant principal at the high school, which requires a lot of unexpected preparations so close to the new school year. But our very good friend Violet Valencia has offered to step in. She's taken care of Melody since she was a baby. I think she's already started packing her bags! She's like family."

I always give smiley faces when it comes to Mrs. V.

"Wonderful!" Marisol said. "Next, I'll be needing

Melody's personal information, things like date of birth, a complete list of any medications, allergies and diet concerns, as well as personal habits and needs. We want to anticipate any situation."

"Yes, of course," Mom said, but then stammered, "B-but Melody on an airplane? Maneuvering through airport security? Going to a major city? I must admit this might be more than our family can handle!"

"Mrs. Brooks, believe me, I understand your concerns. I'm a mom as well. Let's take this one step at a time, okay?"

Mom mumbled something in reply—she was really stressing. But I guess there was an "okay" in that mumble, because Marisol asked if I had a passport.

"Mrs. Valencia has one," Mom said, flustered. "But no, Melody doesn't—We don't do a lot of traveling."

This didn't seem to bother Marisol at all. "Not a problem. I'll email you the application after this phone call, and I'll make sure it gets fast-tracked. Oh, and you'll need to include a passport photo. I've already checked—your local post office can take care of that for you."

Wow! Marisol thought of everything! Mom had pulled out her tablet and was madly jotting down information. I didn't know she could type that fast!

Marisol continued, "Melody and Mrs. Valencia, as well as Miss Gilson and a companion if she chooses, will be booked in first class. A direct flight from Cincinnati, Ohio, is about nine hours. . . ."

And for some reason, that piece of information broke Mom. She gasped. I did too! Then she said, sounding defeated, "This isn't going to work."

"I promise you, Mrs. Brooks, Melody will be treated like royalty, and she will have the experience of a lifetime!"

Mom went quiet, then gathered herself to say, "Give me three reasons why I should let my child, who has some serious life issues, travel to another country."

Instead of answering directly, Marisol surprised us with, "Let me tell you a story, Mrs. Brooks."

"Let her, Mom," I typed.

"When I was in grade school," Marisol began when Mom said to go right ahead. "I read about Helen Keller. She was born in the 1800s. As a toddler, she had a serious illness, probably scarlet fever, and as a result, she was left unable to hear or see, and for a very long time, could not speak."

I was listening intently. I'd heard the name Helen Keller, but that was about it. So I knew what else I'd be researching that week.

Mom, however, said, "Yes, I know her story."

Marisol was smooth. "Great. Then let me tell the both of you a couple of things most people don't know."

I quickly tapped, **"I want to know!"**

"Well, back then, it was really hard to have a child with what we might call 'differences.' These children were often institutionalized or hidden away from society."

"That's terrible!" I tapped.

"Exactly! But Helen, with the encouragement of her teacher, Anne Sullivan, learned to communicate. She traveled all over the world, she wrote books, graduated from college, and even helped to found the American Civil Liberties Union!"

"Really?"

"And that was well before we had computers and the internet. If she could accomplish all that way back when . . . imagine what you can do today!"

My mind was clicking. They for sure didn't have motorized wheelchairs back then. Or probably half the medicines, or machines like Elvira.

Marisol interrupted my mental gymnastics. "While we want to honor Miss Gilson and help her reconnect with her family in London, we also want to honor Melody. But more than that, we want to help plan for Melody's future."

Mom tilted her head. "But . . . why?"

"Fair question," Marisol replied. "This might sound grandiose, but it comes from the heart. We were deeply moved by Melody's own great heart. Your daughter has the potential to make a real difference in the world, to be a light in the darkness for others. Not everyone can step up to that role. But we think—no, we're sure—that Melody can. One step at a time. One person at a time. One adventure at a time. And perhaps that first step is in London at the I.D.E.A. conference."

Mom inhaled. She exhaled. I held my breath.

Then she gave a fierce nod. "Okay, then. Let the world-changing begin!"

My heart beat YES. My brain, not so much. So now I was s'posed to change the world? I frowned. I couldn't even change my own clothes!

CHAPTER 12

Back in my room, I dug into the power of Elvira. First, I looked up plane travel for people with disabilities. Yikes! Apparently, airlines were really good at losing luggage and messing up wheelchairs. Okay, no more looking at that. I had enough to worry about.

So I started searching for everything I could find on Helen Keller. Talk about inspiration! I felt infinitesimally inconsequential compared to her.

I pored over all the photos online: Helen smiling. Helen giving speeches. Helen smelling a rose.

Helen graduating from Radcliffe University—with honors—the first deaf and blind person to do that!

Helen traveling overseas! Take note, Melody!

Helen posing with friends Mark Twain and Alexander Graham Bell. For real?

The more I read, the more awestruck I became.

She was named one of the hundred most important figures of the twentieth century—right up there with Albert Einstein and Mahatma Gandhi!

How did I not know any of this? She even was nominated for the Nobel Peace Prize! And she never heard a single accolade she received. Everything was finger-spelled into the palm of her hand by her teacher. Every single word she wanted to say had to be created the same way. Every. Single. Word.

And I complain about homework and a wheelchair. Jeesh. Imagine what other amazing things she might have accomplished if she'd had something like Elvira!

Which made me think. I figured in seventh grade I'd probably have to write a paper on someone famous, and now I knew who—Helen was my girl! And, yeah, there's lots of stuff I cannot do. But there's lots of stuff that I *can* do. And, okay, so maybe this trip would help me help somebody else, even if it was to let them know they could do more than they thought they could.

I got back on the I.D.E.A. website to make sure I hadn't missed any key info. A lady named Nevaeh Kipfer had started the organization because she felt that movie stars and sports heroes got tons of attention and media coverage, but kids who were academic and scientific geniuses and inventors or exceptional in loads of other ways were mostly overlooked. Go, Navaeh! Now there was a place that basically let these people shine and see what they could achieve!

And, ha! I just noticed this—her name, Nevaeh, was "heaven" spelled backward. Her mother had big dreams for this baby.

But what the website didn't tell me was what these mental megastars could possibly learn from someone like me. I just didn't want to disappoint anybody. Including myself.

CHAPTER 13

After a mostly yummy dinner of mashed potatoes, creamed chicken, and un-yummy peas, I thanked Mom profusely through my board. She looked pleased, then side-eyed me. "So what's that gonna cost me?"

"Two shopping trips and a new suitcase!" I gave an evil laugh, and Butterscotch moved to the safety of the other side of the table. She usually sat right next to me at mealtime because of all the food I dropped.

"Two trips? How come?"

"Because we will forget something important the first time." I'm not wrong!

Dad chuckled, but I could see the worry on his face.

I remembered how nervous he'd been when I'd gone to summer camp, and that was only two hours away. Guess it's Dad's job to worry.

After dinner, I checked ZibberZabber. I was still trending in the top ten. Gee. Plus, there were over a hundred notes and comments, compliments on being on TV, kudos for saving Miss Gertie. Enough already!

But then . . . I saw a new comment. The best one. From Noah. His message read simply, *Proud of you, Firefly Girl!* It was what he'd called me all week at camp.

I fell asleep with a smile on my face.

After list making and remaking and mall shopping and internet searching and even more bagpipe listening, I saw from my window one morning that Miss Gertie was outside, back to tending to her roses. She was whispering to her Tropicanas, probably telling them how gorgeous they were. Yay! That must mean she was feeling lots better.

A pair of blue jays squawked and circled, dive-bombing a squirrel. It must have been trying to get at their feeder, I guessed. Those crests on their heads suited them—they ruled!

Just then a red SUV pulled into Miss Gertie's driveway. I know all the cars of the folks who live around here; this one I'd never seen before. Was it a home care nurse?

A salesperson? Nope, too early. Nosy me kept watching.

A tall, slender teenager almost oozed out of the car. She looked like she was around fourteen. She wore all red, like she had coordinated with the color of the car. Ripped red leggings. An oversized sleeveless T-shirt. And red flip-flops. Her hair, which was just the right amount of messy, looked mega-trendy. Short, pale brown, but sporting a couple of hair spikes—red, of course. She could have walked the runway in a fashion show. Just looking at her made me want to throw away all my clothes and start over.

As the taxi driver unloaded her luggage—a red hard-shell spinner—the girl stretched, then looked around.

Miss Gertie turned from her Tropicanas and waved excitedly. The girl waved back, looking maybe a little uncertain as she rolled her suitcase up the walkway. While Miss Gertie reached out and hugged her tightly, I noticed the girl's hug wasn't quite as enthusiastic. She continued to glance around with what might have been a look of surrender? Resignation? I couldn't tell. They chatted for a minute, then went inside.

Okay, so nosy me was wondering who the heck this girl was—she didn't seem all that happy to be here. But maybe she was just tired.

I knew better than to assume stuff just by looking at

someone. People have always looked at me and assumed all kinds of crazy stuff—like that I'm slow or dumb. And it hurts. So I decided to assume the best about the tall, all-in-red girl.

I stared out my window for the longest time—but they didn't come back out. The suspense was killing me! I couldn't sit there all day, though, so I started looking up cool things to do in London until Penny begged me to watch an episode of *Yabba Dabba Duckie* with her. No lie, I was really glad when our doorbell rang.

Penny dashed off to answer it, even though technically she wasn't allowed to. Mom beat her to it, scolding, "Always wait for Mommy when someone is at the door, Penny."

"Why? I can open it by myself!" she asserted as nosy me wheeled myself over.

"Well, suppose it's a stranger?"

Penny rolled her eyes. "No strangers live around here! Besides, I can see through the glass part of the door. It's Mrs. V . . . aaaannnnd Miss Gertie," she announced. "And, oh, oh, oh! A stranger!" She jumped backward.

Mom swung the door open with a cheery hello. She gave Mrs. V a quick hug, then smoothly slipped her arm through Miss Gertie's, seamlessly escorting her in.

"Welcome to our home, Miss Gilson," she said in her

warmest voice. "Perfect timing! I've just made coffee. Please come in!" She led Miss Gertie to a chair in the kitchen as she said, "What's up, V?"

She then turned to the girl. "And how about you? Would you like some iced tea?" My mom is the best host. She always makes sure everybody has what they need.

The girl said, "No, thank you, ma'am," and leaned against the counter. She looked a little nervous, glanced my way, then glanced away. Okaaay.

"I'm trying to wean myself off coffee," Mrs. V was saying. Then she laughed. "But I'll try harder tomorrow! Today I'll take it with extra cream. Thanks."

Miss Gertie suddenly exclaimed, with her cool British accent, "Where are my manners? Please allow me to introduce my great-niece Skylar Foster. She's visiting me for several weeks. Sky, these are my favorite neighbors— Mrs. Brooks, and her daughters, Melody and Penny. Melody is the young lady who basically saved my life!"

The girl Skylar nodded. She may have mumbled hello or something, but she wasn't going to win a prize for exuberant greetings. She kept her eyes down.

Mom bustled around, pouring coffee for Mrs. V and Miss Gertie, chocolate milk for Penny, and apple juice for me.

Then she turned back to Skylar. "Are you sure you wouldn't like something—chocolate milk, perhaps?"

Skylar looked up at last. "No, thank you. I'm not crazy about chocolate."

Hey, just like me!

Mom nodded. "Let's see, we have apple and orange juice—"

Skylar chose orange juice, and when Mom came back from the fridge, glass in hand, Skylar gulped it down like she hadn't had juice in a hundred years.

Penny watched this juice-gulping feat, then sidled up to her. "Are you named for the whole sky?" she asked.

The girl finally broke into a smile. It was huge, truly cheek to cheek, and she had a tiny gap between her two front teeth.

"Yep, the whole sky! Actually, I like being called just that—Sky."

"Wow. You're lucky." Penny then informed her, "I'm named for just one cent out of a dollar!"

I didn't know she knew that.

"But you are money! Which is pretty cool."

Penny thought about that. "You're right! I am cool! I gotta go tell my Barbies!" She galloped off to her room.

"She's a cutie-pie," Skylar said, finally, to me. "I have a brother, but he's a lot older."

"It must be fun to have a brother," I typed.

"Yeah, Oliver's got an awesome sense of humor, and only teases me, oh, once a week. But I haven't seen him in a while—he's on a year abroad in England, which is a bummer for me." Then she blushed and blurted out, "Okay, so, I gotta admit—I've been following you on ZibberZabber. Girl, you're something!"

I could feel myself blush. I tapped out, **"Everybody is fake-cool on ZZ!"**

We both laughed.

To change the subject, I asked, **"How long are you visiting Miss Gertie?"**

"First, gotta say, your talking board is amazing. Second, I'll be here for at least a month until school starts again in Switzerland." I must have looked confused because she added, "My parents are in the foreign service, and they got called on an emergency trip to Afghanistan— some kind of diplomatic problem." She shrugged.

"Does that happen a lot?" I'd never really heard of families in the foreign service.

"Yep," she said in a no-big-thing voice. "We're always being sent somewhere. I was born in France and raised kind of all over the place, but I've lived in Egypt, Spain, Brazil, India, and Australia."

"WOW" was all I could think to reply. Then I asked, **"Was that fun?"**

She shrugged again. "It's all I've known for the past fourteen years, so basically, my whole life. I've got a big picture of the world and how people live, which is cool.

But the bummer is I've missed the ordinary stuff, like going to the same school for more than a minute, and by the time I make a friend, I know I'm probably going to be leaving again. That kinda sucks."

"Trust me, the school stuff was okay to miss!"

We laughed again. I guess she didn't think talking to me through a speaking device was weird, because she'd experienced so many different things. There was something relaxing about that. I felt chill with her, like I'd known her a long time.

"Can you speak languages other than English?"

"Yep! Three nearly fluently," she admitted.

"I'm learning a bunch too," I tapped out shyly.

"Of course you are! You're the genius who watches TV shows in Arabic—Aunt Gertie outed you!"

"Cool skill. No place to show it off!" I laughed.

Skylar whipped out her phone and tapped a few words on the screen. She looked up to say, "I'm reminding myself to post to the world about Melody the genius— but no pics unless you say it's okay."

I appreciated that. I thought for a second, then tapped, **"I'll trade you: pics of me for you showing me how to post stuff online."**

Her eyes lit up. "Sure, no prob! There're places and sites that will blow your mind. You ever do site bouncing? Or person puddling?"

I'd never even heard of them. **"No, but I really want to!"**

This girl Skylar was pretty cool, I was thinking. I was glad the grown-ups were talking trip logistics, so I could talk to her longer.

It went silent for a moment. Mrs. V is always reminding me to initiate conversations, so I tapped, **"I like your name. It's . . . uh, like freedom!"** Then I felt stupid. Who compliments another kid on their name? I'm such a . . .

But Skylar instantly grinned. "You'd be surprised the crazy things I get called at school, though."

I tapped, **"I bet I got you beat on crazy things people get called at school!"**

We laughed again.

I saw Mom give a head nod to Mrs. V and Miss Gertie, and the three of them slipped quietly out of the kitchen and into the living room with their coffees.

Skylar tilted her head. "Aunt G said you were like super brilliant, and that you saved her life, so, gotta say, I was a little intimidated to meet you."

"I'm just me," I tapped out, my head down.

"Me too," she replied. "Anyway, I'm glad to meet you. It's hard to make friends when you're constantly packing every six months for new positions and locations."

"It can get pretty lonely not going anywhere as well," I admitted.

"Yeah, I bet." Then she asked, "Is it hard to be stuck in that chair?"

"Superglue helps!"

And then we talked forever. About camp (she'd never been), the ocean (I'd never been), and Disney World (neither of us had ever been).

And about boys, too. I told her about Noah, certain that my ears were red. Sky's for sure were as she told me about a guy named Billy Shakespeare at her school in Switzerland.

"Seriously," she said, "if your names are Maude and Gregory Shakespeare, why the heck would you name your son William? Like, don't parents think about teasing?"

I tapped, **"They could have named him Shawn or Michael instead!"**

We both cracked up.

"Maybe he'll grow up to be a famous writer anyway," she added.

He should move to London! I was thinking, which led me to typing: **"So I guess you've heard about me and Miss Gertie and this trip to London?"**

"That's one reason why I'm here. And now that we've met, I'm even more glad I get to go on this trip! And hello, my brother says there's a skillion things to do there!"

Wait—what?

"You're coming with us?!"

She shimmied in her chair. "Aunt Gertie didn't tell you? We're all going together!"

No way! No way! Sky was coming too? My hands started flapping and I kicked the table twice.

CHAPTER 14

We packed. We unpacked. We repacked. We stressed about details and possible problems. We got silly excited. And finally, it was Tuesday, trip day! Penny had been chanting "Tuesday Trip Day" since we got up. Our flight left at six that evening, but we arrived at the airport almost four hours early—Mom wasn't about to risk us being late! I'd missed a flight once before, and for sure we weren't going to let that happen this time.

The terminal was huge and busy, but somehow didn't seem crowded. I marveled at the smooth wheelchair-friendly floors, high ceilings, and organized chaos. Businesspeople cruised along with their rolling suitcases.

Some travelers wore jeans, some sweats, and others were dressed in saris or burkas. It was an international collection of humanity, all heading to another location.

Sky was clearly used to this, but to me, it was amazing!

At the line for security, there were soooooo many tears and goodbyes—Yeah, I got kinda sobby, and Mom was a mess, but Dad was a disaster! Penny just wanted to look at the airplanes out the giant windows. My parents kept waving the whole time us travelers moved through the line, until we could no longer see them!

"I hope they aren't going to stand there waving until I get back," I joked to Sky.

Sky laughed. "I wouldn't be surprised, actually!"

As we made our way to our gate, I started to get a little nervous. Wheelchair users and their families got to board before the rest of the passengers. But we had to switch from our huge, clunky, motorized chairs to what they call a "boarding chair."

A boarding chair is a little like a folding lawn chair— soft, with pretty much no support at all. I slumped in it like a wet noodle. My electric wheelchair was tagged and taken to the hold of the plane where luggage was stored. I gotta say, I felt almost naked without my chair. A naked wet noodle—ha! My chair was part of me, part of how I functioned in the world. I refused, however, to be separated from Elvira. Mom had made sure everybody knew that. Mrs. V carried Elvira for me in a thick knitted bag she'd designed just for this trip.

I was rolled down a long corridor toward the actual door of the plane. Once inside, my breath caught. It was massive, with rows and rows of blue seats stretching from the front to waaaay in the back, and lots of seats across. I'd looked it up—the plane could hold up to three hundred people. That was more than my whole school!

Above me were overhead bins—open and ready to be stuffed with carry-on bags and backpacks. Because the studio had booked us first-class seats—*ooh la la*—Mrs. V and I were seated in seats 1A and 1B on the left, and Sky and Miss Gertie's seats were 1C and 1D on the right. Sky and I had aisle seats—in the front of the plane—boom!

Mrs. V showed me how the seats reclined—all the way flat like a bed. We even had blankets and pillows and little slippers! Zowee! This was fancier than I even imagined.

As Mrs. V shifted me out of the wet noodle chair and into my "throne," as she jokingly called it, other passengers boarded the seats behind us. A flight attendant, dressed in a kinda cute gray uniform, stopped at our seats. Her smile was warm and friendly, like she was truly happy to see us.

"Welcome to Delta, your home away from home. Would you like some juice or fruit or nuts? We have pecans and cashews today, and our choice of juices are orange, cranberry, apple, and passion fruit. But we also have soft drinks and water if you prefer."

Okay, I was totally impressed! Sky and Miss Gertie ordered cranberry juice, and Mrs. V ordered passion-fruit juice for us. I was feeling a little self-conscious about having to be fed on the plane, but the attendants barely glanced our way. They probably saw stuff like that all the time.

Mrs. V tucked a blanket around me, and I happily observed a seemingly endless stream of people as they boarded. It was almost like watching a movie.

—a young mother with a toddler in one arm and an infant in a baby carrier strapped to her chest

—a bearded man in a fedora

—a nun wearing a white collar and a long blue habit

—three men in sleek black suits

—a woman with dozens of very long black braids past her butt

—a teenager with a Cincinnati Reds baseball cap on backward, wearing a Reds jersey too

—two super-skinny college-age girls wearing SAVE THE WHALES shirts

—an elderly woman with a cane in her right

hand, and an elderly man with a cane in his left hand directly behind her. They held on to each other's free hand.

—a very large man who wore so much cologne that people coughed when he passed

—a young woman wearing a dressy white pullover that said BRIDE. She looked delighted.

—a young man right behind her wearing a black T-shirt that said GROOM. He looked tired. That made me giggle.

It took twenty minutes for everyone to board, find their seats, stuff their luggage into overhead compartments, and settle into the place where they'd be sitting for a very long time.

No one seemed stressed or worried. Except maybe me, and I kept it all inside. Number one, I worried about going to the bathroom. Number two, I was nervous about eating and sleeping on a plane. Number three, I worried about whether pilots got tired or sleepy. Then I started to worry about crashing, about landing. . . . Okay, I had to get myself together! *People do this every single day. Relax and enjoy this, Melody!* So that's what I decided to do.

A flight attendant grabbed a microphone and clicked on the public address system. Mrs. V grabbed my hand. This was it!

"Ladies and gentlemen, welcome aboard Flight 1948 with nonstop service from Cincinnati, Ohio, to London's Heathrow Airport. You are flying in a lovely Boeing 767 jet, and our flight time will be approximately eight hours and twenty-five minutes."

I looked up. That was nearly NINE hours! I mean, I *knew* that, but it hadn't fully registered.

Note to self: There is no way you can go nine hours without having to go to the bathroom. Nine hours is forever! I thought about that mother I just saw with two little kids. Penny couldn't sit still for ten minutes! How could a toddler?

But I reminded myself that I was nearly a teenager, invited to be a part of an international symposium. I can deal with this. Ha! I guess I kinda have to!

The flight attendants did one last seat-belt check, which made me think that right now, three hundred people were just like me, strapped into seat belts, having absolutely no control of their situation. That was either terrifying or comforting—I wasn't sure which! Maybe— ha-ha—BOTH!

Finally, with a rush of noise and acceleration, the plane began to move. At first, slowly, where I could see every airport building, to faster, then so fast everything outside the window became a blur.

Then suddenly, as if it were a bird leaving its nest, the

plane was no longer on the ground! Trees and airport buildings shrank as we rose. I could feel the surge of power as the plane went up, up, up. Faster and faster. I would say as swift as a bird, but the fastest bird in the universe (a hawk, I think) couldn't fly fast enough to keep up with this metallic bird we were riding in.

Weird, though, 'cause I couldn't feel the speed. My ears felt funny, so I forced myself to swallow, and I felt them pop a little. But to be honest, I hardly felt any difference between being on this jet and being in Mom's car.

I looked over at Sky. She gave me a double thumbs-up. We were on our way—to London!

CHAPTER 15

We had no time to get bored. There were snacks, more snacks, and the promise of a full meal, and did any of us want champagne! The flight attendant winked when she said this, then offered more juice to me and Sky. Mom had spent eons telling the airline about my dietary needs, so each time a food was brought out, a version had been prepared just for me. When Sky ordered steak, I got an egg-sausage-creamed hash, which was delicious. Even the muffins had been prepared so that I could easily eat them.

No complaints here.

After dinner was whisked away, Sky and I checked out

the screens in front of us, which had billions of choices: about fifty movies and oodles of other videos (including airplane exercises—no thank you!); sports stations; recent and old-time television shows; and dozens of music channels, from country music to jazz. No one could blame the airline if we got bored!

Mrs. V swapped seats with Sky—bet she knew I'd have more fun that way. She's so good to me. Sky and I breathed a sigh of relief and checked out a fashion channel, a food channel, and a show we had to pause so I could type to Sky, **"Didja see how fine that dude is?"**

"Oh yeah!" She burst out laughing, and I did too.

Maybe it was the food, but soon we couldn't keep our eyes open. We reclined the seats all the way flat. Mrs. V made sure we were snuggled with our pillows and blankets, then dimmed the lights above our heads. Sky zonked out first, blanket around her head like a cloak. I was so sleepy, but at the same time soooo jazzed that I couldn't actually fall asleep, so I watched the screen that showed exactly where the airplane was in the air. We were over the Atlantic Ocean now! Wow! And before I knew it, I dozed off.

I woke up not sure how long I'd slept. Sky was snoring soft little snores. Miss Gertie was snoozing as well. Mrs. V, however, was wide awake, leafing through a magazine and watching a movie at the same time.

"You good, Melody?" she asked when she saw I was awake.

I nodded.

"Is this not the best adventure in the galaxy?"

I gave her a huge grin.

She looked around the quiet cabin, then asked, "Do you need to use the bathroom?"

I shook my head. But my brain was saying, *Hello! No way are you going to be able to hold out until the end of the flight.* Then it occurred to me that going now, while most of the passengers were asleep, would attract the least attention. That thought was followed by a surge of sadness as I was reminded, yet again, that I would always need someone to help me in the bathroom, to help me with bathing and dressing and eating. Always.

I blinked away tears. I couldn't even think about what it was going to be like when I was a full-on teenager and my body started going through big-time changes.

"Let's scoot in now while folks are asleep," Mrs. V suggested with a wink.

I nodded glumly. She whispered something to a flight attendant, who reached into a tall, thin closet and pulled out the soft-bottomed boarding chair. Like she'd done since I was a baby, Mrs. V lifted me from my seat to that chair, whooshed me to the restroom, let me take care of business, washed my hands, and had me back in my seat so easily that if there were an award for efficiency, effectiveness, and discreetness, she would have won it.

I reached out my arms and gave her the biggest hug I could squeeze out. I wanted to shout, *Thank you, thank you, for all you've done for me!* But all I could do was squeeze. It was enough. She knew.

CHAPTER 16

I must have fallen asleep again, because when I next opened my eyes, Sky said, "About time, girl!"

Which made me think—time in the air kinda meant nothing. Whole time zones below us were zipping by in moments, seconds, hours. And into "infinity and beyond," as Penny would remind me about Buzz Lightyear. Time around *us* could only be counted by how long we'd been flying. And time above us was the sky eternal, which simply existed between day and night. I needed to remember to tell Penny all this!

Mrs. V had just finished adjusting the seat so I could

sit up more when a cute bearded flight attendant stopped to ask, "Would you ladies like some ice cream?"

Who wouldn't want ice cream? Sky and I nodded at the same time. "Absolutely! Two please," she politely requested.

"Vanilla or coffee or strawberry?" he asked.

Sky didn't even have to check with me—she knew.

"All three!" She gave him her *I'm so cute* smile.

"You betcha," he said with a little bow.

While we waited for the ice cream, it occurred to me that, duh, I couldn't feed myself! And Mrs. V was finally asleep. My leg kicked out in frustration. But when the flight attendant returned, he had included extra spoons, and lots of extra napkins. Sky took a taste first.

"Scrumptiously delicious!" she asserted.

Then she took a fresh spoon and spooned a bit of the strawberry ice cream into my mouth like she'd done it all her life. I slurped that coolness in and knew in that moment that I truly had a friend.

CHAPTER 17

One meal later—breakfast this time—I could see sunrise out the window. And after one more quick bathroom visit, I came back to find that Sky was packing up her backpack.

Suddenly it seemed that everyone was in a rush. The flight attendants strode through the aisles, collecting trays and tossing leftovers. People put up their tray tables and moved their seats upright. The energy felt different somehow, like how Butterscotch gets when she knows we're about to turn the corner onto our street. Giddy anticipation. Nervous excitement. It was hard to believe we'd been flying for over eight hours. We'd left on Tuesday, and now it was Wednesday!

Mrs. V double-checked her purse for our passports and paperwork. Miss Gertie stared out the window, smiling, as if she could recognize the shape of London clouds.

"What time is it?" I tapped to Mrs. V.

"London is five hours ahead of us. So it's two in the morning at home, but it's seven in the morning here. It will feel weird for a day or so until your body catches up with the change in time zone."

I could have asked how, but I honestly didn't want a lesson on time zones and earth rotation. The only time zone that mattered right now was the one I was in—London's!

CHAPTER 18

We landed with a thud, a *long* roll, and a whoosh as the plane slowed down. Everyone clapped. Were they thanking the pilots?

I looked out the window and saw, uh, England! Well, what I saw was an airport, but this one was in another country on another continent! Even though I imagine all airports look about the same, somehow this one felt different—like magical possibilities awaited ahead.

Everyone grabbed their carry-on bags and stuff from the overhead bins, hustling and bustling cheerfully, and began moving off the plane. We had to wait for my wheelchair—they were going to bring it right up to the door of the plane for me. We waited. And waited.

The co-pilot got off, then even the captain. She tipped her hat to us, grabbed her captain's bag, and left. Nobody seemed to be concerned about the whereabouts of my wheelchair. Uh, I kinda needed that thing.

Sky looked around, a little concerned. "Shouldn't Melody's chair be here by now? Or at least that chair we used before?"

Just then a tall skinny man in a uniform rushed over to us with the boarding chair. We grabbed our stuff, hurried out of the plane, and then . . . nothing. All the rest of the passengers had headed to their gates and destinations, and suddenly, the area was deserted.

What do I do now? I thought helplessly.

As the cleaning crew headed in, another uniformed man finally appeared, wheeling my chair with one hand. I felt ridiculously happy to see my chair, like reuniting with an old friend.

But my stomach clenched up when he said, "Uh, there might have been just a wee bit of damage during the flight."

"Excuse me?" Mrs. V said archly. "There certainly better not be any damage!"

"Sorry, ma'am. I just bring up the chairs to the passengers. You'll need to see a gate agent about any problems." He locked the chair brakes, hesitated for just a moment, then shrugged and hurried off.

What the heck?

My chair was a mess.

The left armrest dangled dangerously.

The right armrest looked twisted.

The back cushion was scratched. I grunted at Mrs. V—My chair! What if I couldn't use my chair! No, I wasn't going to panic.

At least the wheels, as far as I could tell, were all still connected. I think.

Mrs. V, her don't-mess-with-me face back on, stomped off. She was back three minutes later with a man carrying a toolbox.

"Welcome to London!" he said cheerily, despite Mrs. V staring daggers. "Lovely chair you have there, m'dear," he told me. "I don't want even one of your memories of London to be negative, so give me a moment and let's see what the trouble is."

He pulled a few tools out of the box. He adjusted levers and found screws to reattach the dangling armrest.

I could tell Mrs. V was really upset, but she said nothing. The man gave each armrest one last shake to make sure each was on tightly, then double-checked the wheels and motor as well.

Then, with a flourish toward Mrs. V, he said, "Please have a go over, ma'am, and see if it's working to your satisfaction. I've got a wee one at home who needs a bit of help getting about, so I know how important this is to you both."

Mrs. V suddenly looked close to tears. "We can't thank you enough, sir!" She swiftly transferred me to my wheelchair, checked the forward, back, turn, and stop controls, and boom, I was back in business! When Mrs. V shook his hand, I know for sure that the guy received a hefty, well-deserved tip.

With our first emergency now averted, Miss Gertie said grandly, "Now, on to baggage claim and customs so we can be officially admitted to England!"

Customs was a breeze. Because of me and the wheel-chair, we were able to zoom past the crowds. For once, *I* made things quicker. My passport was stamped, and next thing I heard was "Welcome to London!"

CHAPTER 19

Waiting in the taxi queue (a British word I just learned that means "line") with our luggage, I could hardly sit still. I gulped down air—this was the same air breathed by Queen Elizabeth and Shakespeare! I tried to look everywhere at once. In front of us were red double-decker buses—so cute they could have been toys—and shiny black cabs, much bigger than the yellow ones at home.

Mrs. V found a cab for us in no time. And guess what? The cab had a built-in wheelchair ramp! The driver told us that *all* the London black cabs had them. All. Of. Them. Major points for London! USA, are you listening?

Our cabbie, whose name was Sebastian—so British!—

piled our luggage into the back, got us loaded in, and pointed out various sites as we headed to our hotel. Cathedrals and a castle; museums and monuments—zowie! One I recognized even before Sebastian pointed it out: Big Ben, an enormous clock on top of a three-hundred-foot tower.

Miss Gertie had her face pressed against the window like a little kid. "That clock was built over a hundred and fifty years ago, and no, I wasn't around then," she told us with a laugh. "The face of it is made from hundreds of individual pieces of glass."

"Impressive," Sky agreed. "So, you'd have to climb over three hundred steps to get to the top!"

"No thank you!" I tapped on my board.

Sky elbowed me, laughing. "I hear you!"

"Did you know London is twice as big as New York?"

"We're going to be doing *lots* of walking," Sky said decidedly.

Mrs. V peered out the window. "I hope the day stays lovely for us." Did I mention the sky was blue-jay blue, and the sun seemed to practically be greeting us, it was beaming so brightly? None of that rain London was so famous for. My heart was thrumming with excitement.

The other thing I immediately noticed was that streets were set up exactly the opposite from the US. At home, we drive on the right side of the road, but in England folks drive on the left. I kept worrying that cars would drive into us, or us into them. But nope. Everybody had it down except me, I guess. Ha. I wondered how my dad would handle driving here. Bet it would take some getting used to.

After passing about ten more monuments, we finally pulled up to the gates of the Marlington Hotel. The hotel was enormous, made of gray bricks and stones. A curved drive led to gleaming wooden doors so wide our cab could have driven through them. I gaped. It was practically a castle!

Sky and I were having a mind-meld moment, because she said, "I love how some hotels here look like castles!"

I grinned in agreement.

Check-in was easy-peasy, and moments later we were in an elevator, where the bellhop with our luggage asked us what floor we wanted. Miss Gertie gave him the number. "Brilliant views from that floor, ma'am," he said proudly.

"Are we all staying in the same room?" Sky asked. I wondered that as well.

"Yes, but we asked for two king-size beds," Mrs. V said. "One for the two old folks and one for the two young ones." She paused and smirked. "Unless you two want to sleep with the elders!"

Sky looked to me and made a silly face. "Oh, we're

good, thank you. Melody and I have tons to talk about."
Our elevator shuddered to a stop. The man announced
our floor and gave a slight bow as we exited.

Our room was . . . ginormous. Sky immediately
bounced on one of the beds, while the first thing I
checked out was the bathroom. Yep, wheelchair accessible. Phew! There were paintings of different London
parks on the walls, and if we got tired of the paintings,
we could just look out the window—at a massive park,
with flowers everywhere. I'd need to ask Sky to take a
photo for me to show Mom.

Just as the bellhop finished unloading our suitcases
off the luggage cart and left, the doorbell rang. (Yes, our
room had a doorbell!) Mrs. V opened the door and two
waiters, *dressed in tuxedos,* swept in with two giant trays of
food!

"G'day, ladies," the first waiter said crisply. "We've prepared some bubble and squeak for ya, to welcome you to
London! We've heard we have a celebrity in our midst,
and it's her favorite meal." *Wow,* I thought—Channel 12
thought of everything! But what the heck was bubble
and squeak?

I quickly typed, **"What a cool name for a food! What
is it?"**

"Fried potatoes and cabbage, although originally it
was beef and cabbage. My grandmama made it every

holiday," Miss Gertie told us, clapping her hands. "The Scottish name for it is rumbledethumps! Not one's traditional breakfast meal, but we had breakfast on the plane."

Mrs. V thanked the waiters enthusiastically, and they bowed out of the room. Each plate sat under a little silver dome. Just as I was starting to worry as I saw the thick wedges of bubble and squeak—too chunky for me to eat—Mrs. V lifted the last dome, and yay, there was the same food, but pureed and in a sparkling clear bowl. My first British meal, and it was delicious. Wait till I told Penny about rumbledethumps! She'd love that word.

We decided to head out into the city after eating— Miss Gertie said that the best way to avoid jet lag was to force yourself to stay awake and follow the time in the country you were in. Fine by me. I was way too excited to take a nap.

We pored through the list of London highlights that Sky and I had compiled on the plane and I'd saved in a file on Elvira. Mrs. V also had something like ten guidebooks with different titles, all of them different versions of *Stuff to Do in London*. We picked the changing of the guard at Buckingham Palace to see first—Miss Gertie thought that would be the perfect start to our adventure. Sky and I hoped we would spy some royalty, but I guess the royals don't just wander the streets of London!

On our way out we made a quick stop at the hotel gift shop to buy some cool shades and silly straw hats because it was so sunny and warm out. Sky insisted I get a bright red hat, of course; it had a huge brim and a bold yellow sash around it. She chose one that looked like something Sherlock Holmes would wear, with a brim on both ends and flaps that tied up at the ears—except I doubt that Sherlock had a picture of the queen. Yep, we were now official tourists!

CHAPTER 20

"The changing of the guard starts precisely at ten forty-five, so we should head over straightaway," Miss Gertie said as the bellhop flung out an arm to get a cab's attention.

Crowds had already started to gather when our cab deposited us at Buckingham Palace. BTW, I couldn't *believe* I'm tossing around phrases like "Buckingham Palace" and the "royal guard"! I also couldn't believe how many people were here to watch.

We wiggled into a spot near the front, and whoa, there they were! Bright red coats. Crisp white belts. Perfectly pressed black pants. Highly shined black boots.

And their hats—I was obsessed! They were really tall, rounded at the top, and Miss Gertie told us they were made of bearskin. The guards carried rifles—I had no idea if they were real or loaded, but they sure looked impressive. The two guards in front had actual gleaming silver swords.

"Nobody's going to mess with those guys," Sky whispered to me.

"For sure not me," I tapped. As if they were tapping back, drums started beating. Trumpets sounded! A guard wearing a hat even taller than the others bellowed an order. The guards on one side shifted their rifles to the opposite arm, the guards on the other side shifted their rifles in the opposite way, and they started marching. Left. Right. Left. Right. Not one footstep out of place. Their arms swung out in perfect unison. They stared straight ahead, their faces fierce, not even glancing at the crowd. I wondered how many hours they had to practice to get that good.

Left. Right. Stomp. Stomp. Black and red and white and gold. Absolute precision.

"Awesome!" I tapped.

Sky yelled into my ear over the music, "What if they get an itch? Or trip on a rock? What if they have to sneeze?!"

"No sneezing allowed. Straight to the dungeon!" Sky

laughed and we edged closer. As the guards came to a halt just a dozen feet from us, I could smell a strong funky horse smell—kind of a mix between sweat and polish. I hadn't noticed that police on horseback were, well, guarding the guards from the crowd.

Just then, a chestnut-colored horse stopped right beside me. I thought of the horse that had taken me on a joyride at camp; no way would the stern-looking police officer riding this one would ever let something like that happen. And whoa, was this horse huge. I gazed up as the police officer gazed out at the crowd, hand over his eyes because of the sun. The horse shifted just a teeny bit closer. Then closer. Then *eek!* I felt my hat leave my head!

The horse had grabbed it! It began munching on it like I did my morning cereal!

Sky, and several other people, pointed and laughed out loud. "I guess your hat looked like the breakfast of champions!"

The police officer looked aghast. "Silvino, no!" he scolded, reaching forward to save my hat. The horse shook its head out of reach, and half the hat disappeared into its mouth. "My apologies, young lady," the police officer said as he nudged the horse away. I wanted to tell him no worries but was too busy giggling. Sky snapped a photo of the last of my hat as they moved on along the crowd.

"I'm sorry about your hat," Miss Gertie said. "Our horses are usually better behaved!"

"No worries," I tapped. **"It was red. Maybe he thought it was a giant apple!"**

As the guards being relieved of duty march off to, well, I don't know where exactly—did they go take naps?—Mrs. V asked if we wanted to go inside the palace itself. The outside was beautiful, made of stone so creamy and luxurious-looking that I could hardly imagine what the inside looked like. Sky suggested watching the balcony in case some royals came out, but Miss Gertie told us they only did that on special occasions. Did my hat getting eaten by a royal horse count? Ha. Probably not.

But did we want to go INSIDE? Um, you know we did!! "Don't we need tickets ahead of time?" Sky asked. Miss Gertie very mysteriously dug around in her handbag, then pulled out an envelope with a flourish, giving a sly nod to Mrs. V.

"Tickets?!" I tapped.

"With step-free wheelchair access!" Miss Gertie said triumphantly. "You can go just about anywhere any other tourist can go to. There are a lot of steps throughout the palace, but you can take special lifts to circumvent them."

I was stunned. So was Sky. She gushed a thank-you exactly as I was typing the same.

"Thank Channel 12," Miss Gertie said. "Now, shall we enter the palace, m'ladies?"

I couldn't help but wonder, was seeing a prince included in the ticket? Heh-heh.

CHAPTER 21

My wheelchair was checked and checked again by very serious-looking men making sure I wasn't sneaking anything dangerous into the palace, which, hello, did they not see I couldn't hold a guidebook, never mind anything harmful? Then there we were, rolling through room after room, more sumptuous, gilded, and garnished than I'd ever imagined.

I tried to take mental notes to remember to tell my parents when I got home, but it was impossible. Would I tell them that there were paintings *everywhere*, even on the ceilings? Or how massive the windows were (imagine cleaning those, no thank you!), or how all the furniture was super-duper fancy with tassels hanging from the bottoms, and chandeliers dangling from every ceiling? There was a music room—yes, a room just for listening to music in. It was as big as our entire house, with a gleaming gold piano at one end that had cupids painted on the side, and legs that curled at the bottom like a lion's paw. Ohhhh, I was aching to touch those piano keys. A guard might have been reading my mind, as he watched me carefully as I wheeled closer. Or maybe he was worried I'd lose control of my wheelchair and crash into the piano. They'd probably kick me out of England for that!

We even got to see the throne room. Sky was in heaven.

"Everything is red! The walls, the carpet . . ." She took picture after picture to show her mom exactly how she wanted her bedroom redecorated. "This room is fire!" she declared, finally putting her phone away. I wondered how often the queen had used this room. It was pretty neat to know that she'd been in the very same room I was now in, and not so long ago! Though I have to say, the throne looked pretty . . . uncomfortable. Definitely not ergonomic, like *my* "throne."

Buckingham Palace has 775 rooms, and 78 bathrooms, and yep, we used one of those. The handicapped one was so fancy, I almost couldn't go! The room I liked best was named the White Drawing Room. It wasn't the biggest, but as I twirled my chair around and around, it felt a bit like I was inside a wedding cake turned inside out. Plus, ohhhhhh, it had a secret door! Miss Gertie explained the reason for it, because—and here she made our minds explode—she had once met with the queen in this room! I guess even queens like to meet other celebrities. And apparently, there were secret doors that the queen entered rooms from, since most of where she lived in the palace were her "private quarters": areas regular people, or even celebrities, weren't allowed into. I got that. Everyone needed downtime, even queens.

"So she just almost magically made her entrance in the middle of the room!" Miss Gertie was saying. Kind of like something out of Harry Potter—or Narnia, I was thinking. "See if you can spy where that door might be!"

Sky and I searched the room up and down, but it was impossible to find. Then, as I took a last lap around the perimeter, I noticed that one massive, nearly floor-to-ceiling mirror, with a cabinet in front of it, was sticking out just the tiniest bit more than the other identical mirrors in the room did. My legs did their kick thing and I gave a squeal-squawk. A guard nearby looked over and winked. I'd found it! How fun that must be, to be able to sneak around in secret passages and pop into random rooms and surprise visitors. It was a good thing Penny wasn't here—she'd have found some way to sneak in. Then she'd get kicked out of England too.

So. Out of 775 rooms, I think we made it through seven. Seven rooms equaled thirty-one chandeliers; yep, I was counting. But it was way past lunchtime, and Miss Gertie was looking a little tired. She wondered if her favorite fish-and-chip shop was still in business. It was just a short walk from the palace to where the restaurant was, she said. If we could have "a wee sit" in the park in front of the palace, she'd be "right as rain."

CHAPTER 22

Miss Gertie had another surprise for us once we crossed from the palace to St. James's Park. Instead of ducks swimming in the lake in the center, there were . . . pelicans!

Yep, pelicans. In the water and strutting along the edge. They looked like fuzzy, downy dinosaur-birds. With their long, skinny, curvy necks and equally long, skinny bills, I wondered how they managed to eat. Yet as they paddled on the greenish murk, they looked surprisingly graceful, even serene, like they might actually fall asleep while floating. Apparently, the queen loved pelicans.

Miss Gertie sank onto a marble bench while the rest

of us snuck closer. We were able to get so close I felt like I could touch them. But I didn't—for sure. One, however, waddled over and stared right at me, as if I were the exotic, beautiful one. I willed my legs not to kick. Did pelicans bite? I didn't want to find out.

"My father used to bring me here when I was a girl," Miss Gertie sang out dreamily. "There've been pelicans here for three hundred years—apparently a Russian ambassador brought the first ones as a present to the king."

Pretty memorable present, I thought.

"And around the corner you'll see some of the queen's swans," she added.

"Why are they the queen's?" I tapped.

"All the swans in England—well, the ones called mute swans—belong to the Crown, have for over five hundred years! Dolphins, as well."

"What! *All* the swans in the whole country? And dolphins? But how come?" Sky asked.

"Ah, for a very good reason, not to worry." Miss Gertie waved an arm toward the birds. "To keep them from being harmed by poachers."

"Well, I'll allow that," Sky said with her best attempt at a British accent, which was quite good, actually.

Sure enough, we turned past some bushes, and six swans came sailing by. They looked positively regal—it wouldn't have surprised me if there were crowns on their heads. Farther in toward the center of the lake were three black swans too! They looked just as royal. Sky was seriously going to run out of space on her phone, and it was only our first day!

I touched my board and asked, **"Are there any blue jays here?"**

Miss Gertie thought for a moment. "Not as many as we have at home, but yes, I remember seeing some near our house when I was a child."

I thought about the jays in Mrs. V's yard—so very far away. Was it possible for a bird to fly from the US across the ocean to England? I doubted it. So how did birds from the same species end up so far away from each other? Maybe I'd look that up on Elvira this evening. But it was fun to think that cousins of the birds I loved watching at home lived here as well—probably chirping with a British accent!

Just then, a pelican swooped over our heads, the tail of a fish just visible in its beak. *What a wingspan,* I thought.

"Time for fish-and-chips" was what Mrs. V thought, out loud. And we all agreed.

CHAPTER 23

It turned out that Miss Gertie's favorite fish-and-chip shop, Finley's Fish & Chips, was exactly where she remembered it. And it turned out chips aren't potato chips. They're even better . . . they're French fries! I can't really eat potato chips, but I hadn't wanted to make a fuss, so I was extra glad about this.

The restaurant was packed, a lot of people getting their food to go, or what Miss Gertie called "takeaway." The menu had a lot on it besides fish-and-chips—jellied eel, peas literally called "mushy peas" (not a pea fan, but I had to check these out), and, get this: toad-in-the-hole. I was NOT going to try jellied eel, thank you very much, but what the heck was a toad-in-the-hole?

Luckily, we got a table immediately, and as we waited for our order, I kept noticing people getting takeaway were being handed packets wrapped in newspaper.

"What's in the newspaper?" I had to ask.

"Oh! That's the traditional way of packaging fish-and-chips for takeaway," she told us.

Sky frowned. "In newspaper?"

"Oh, yes. You see, the fish-and-chips are fried, and therefore very greasy. Wrapping them in newspaper absorbs the grease while keeping the food warm until you get home, so it stays nice and crispy."

"Is the newspaper new?" Sky asked.

"Of course, fresh from the printer."

So . . . I wasn't sure I'd like fish-and-chips, but Mrs. V mashed some up for me and said I only had to try one bite; if I didn't like it, there was a side of mushy peas waiting for me. And I wasn't even done eating when I was already saying we needed to have fish-and-chips every night for dinner.

Miss Gertie heartily agreed. "I love many American dishes, but nothing hits the spot like perfectly crisped fish-and-chips."

Sky was braver than me. She tried the toad-in-the-hole, which turned out to be thick sausage wrapped in something called Yorkshire pudding. She proclaimed it delish, so Mrs. V mashed a bit up for me as well. I proclaimed it delish too. So then I got even braver and tried the mushy peas, and YUM. Turned out they're a different type of pea than I'd had before, sweeter, and mushed to perfection.

As soon as she finished eating, Sky insisted on hearing more about Miss Gertie's meeting with the queen.

Miss Gertie fluttered both hands in the air as if to wave away the request. "Oh, that's ancient history."

"We're here to discover ancient history!" Mrs. V coaxed.

Miss Gertie glanced around, as if someone might overhear, then low-voiced, "Well, if you insist."

"We insist," I tapped.

We all leaned close. It turned out Miss Gertie had been invited as part of a small audience to meet with the queen after a play Miss Gertie had been in—*A Midsummer Night's Dream*—with an actor named Laurence somebody won some major award. And the award they won is now named after this Laurence guy! And the queen wanted to meet him, and he brought some of the cast with him. And that's how Miss Gertie had tea with the queen.

"Oh, she was lovely, she was," Miss Gertie cooed. "Not tall at all, yet her presence radiated throughout the room. And she asked each of us the most penetrating questions. As if she truly wanted to know the answers."

Miss Gertie looked off into the distance, clearly remembering. "Think of all the people she had to meet in a day, a week, a year, a decade, yet she took the time to learn about us. My goodness!"

"Did she tell *you* anything?" Sky wanted to know, nibbling on the last of my chips.

"Well, she told me that she loved to dance, and she wanted to know when I'd started lessons."

"You used to dance?!" I typed.

"Oh yes, my dear. Back then, most actresses had to."

I thought about that. I had never really thought of what Miss Gertie's "before" might have been like. I wondered if she missed dancing. And then I wondered if you missed something more if you had it and then didn't have it or if you never had it in the first place. At camp we did wheelchair dancing, and I'd never even known you could do that! But once I tried it, I couldn't wait to do it again. So, huh. It's a good thing Mrs. V said we had time to slip in one more bit of fun before heading back to our hotel, or my brain might have gone into protest thinking those thoughts!

CHAPTER 24

Sky read from our Gotta Do list we'd made on the plane. "The Tower of London. Westminster Abbey. The British Museum! The Wallace Collection, where they keep the armor and swords!"

I wondered if folks who lived here visited these places, or was it just tourists like us?

Sky paused and drummed the table. "Let's gooooo! They all sound great."

"Wait, there's lots more!" I tapped.

So Sky kept reading. "The Harry Potter place! Bubble Planet! The London Library! The London Eye. A play!"

"Hold on there, we'll be here till Christmas to cover all of this," Mrs. V exclaimed with a smile.

"Okay by me!" I tapped.

"We'll get in as many as we can," she promised. "But let's pick one for now."

Miss Gertie gave an unexpected little shriek. "Oh, I must bring you to Hatchards. Put that on the list." When we all looked at her quizzically, she explained that it was probably the oldest surviving bookstore in London. "Queen Charlotte used to shop there, back in the 1800s! Stepping in there is truly like stepping back in time."

It must have been fascinating to live here back then, I thought as I rolled slowly down the wide sidewalks, our bill paid. Then I remembered how, "back in the day," as Mrs. V would say, folks tossed the contents of their "chamber pots" out the window each morning. Basically, they threw their pee onto the sidewalk! Maybe onto this very sidewalk. Ewwwww. Guess having some things go out of style is a good thing.

"It's such a clear day," Mrs. V was saying. "Let's take advantage of it. Shall we see if we can ride the London Eye?"

Sky fist-pumped. "Yaaaaaaah! Melody and I just read about it last night!" It was like a ginormous Ferris-wheel-looking ride, a giant circle in the center of the city, but instead of seats, you rode in these dangling bubble-like pods that you could walk around in and see in every direction.

"It will give us a bird's-eye view of the layout of the city," Mrs. V added. Miss Gertie was eager as well; it hadn't existed when she'd lived here.

We totally lucked out—some tourist group cancelled last-minute, so Miss Gertie snapped up four tickets, and Mrs. V rolled me up the platform and right into one of the enormous glass capsules. Penny had always been fascinated with blowing bubbles. This was like I was being transported inside a giant glass one! I could hardly wait to tell her.

The pod was huge—plenty of room for me to roll around in my chair, with a bench in the middle if Miss Gertie needed to sit. We were completely encased in curved glass. Once everyone had boarded our pod— fifteen other people—the wheel started moving, so gently that I hardly felt it.

As we rose above the city, I could see the cars below, tiny and toylike. And the river—the Thames—looked more and more like a ribbon the higher we got, with tiny boats filled with tiny people riding in them. And ooh, a tiny Big Ben. It was like London had turned into a Lego town.

I thought the pod would rock in the wind, the way a seat on a Ferris wheel would, but it was as still as could be.

Sky and I could roam from one end of the pod to the other, looking out for what seemed like miles. A gull drifted alongside us, as interested in us as we were in him. We were side by side with a flying gull! We were so close I could even see a little chip in its beak. Not something this wheelchair-riding girl ever expected. The bird made flying seem so easy. If only.

"Oh, look, there's a castle!" Sky cried out, pointing past the gull. It was so far away it looked straight out of a fairy tale. A teenage boy beside us, who kept glancing at Sky, told us that it was Windsor Castle, and you could see it only on the clearest days. We totally lucked out again!

I thought of my friend Noah. His favorite places were amusement parks—he said he craved the rush of the rides. He would have loved this. So, without overthinking it, I tapped his number. Incredibly, on the first ring, he picked up!

"What's up, Firefly Girl?" he asked, sounding happy to hear from me, and not even surprised.

"I'm in England! On the London Eye! So I had to call!" I tapped quickly.

"London? The London Eye? Amazing! That thing's crazy high!" he raved. "Are you loving it or scared?"

"A little of both." It was true!

Then, as if being asked out by a boy happened to me every day, he said all casually, "Labor Day weekend. You and me. Cedar Point Park. The Millennium Force giga coaster."

Whoa! I'd heard of that coaster. A few words came to mind: Terrifying. Awesome. Fierce.

He piled on some more. "Longest drop. Fastest speed. Hits ninety-three miles per hour! You game for the challenge?"

"Front row?"

"You know it!"

"Challenge accepted! See you!"

The call dropped then, but it was enough. Noah was glad to hear from me! And yep, I was ready to take on that roller-coaster ride.

It was hard to get my head around the fact that we were moving and yet we couldn't tell we were moving, except when we moved ourselves to change up our views. On the airplane, there were bumps here and there, but here, the ride was slow, smooth, and silent. Sky and I again found ourselves next to the boy who'd told us about Windsor Castle. He seemed to be with his father—they had the same red hair—and a little sister who shrieked "Wowsie, wowsie, wowsie!" every time a bird flew close.

Sky said, "Your sister is so cute!"

I kinda envied how easily she fell into conversation with him; he was pretty cute himself.

He looked down at his sister and made a funny face.

"Thanks. She can be a handful when she doesn't like something. But she's really into this. Is it your first time on the Eye? Are you here alone?"

Sky actually blushed. Then she told him, "Yeah, first time, and I've never been on anything like it! I'm here with my friend Melody." She pointed at me.

When the boy glanced down, his eyes widened. A string of drool was slipping down my chin; my wheelchair was glinting in the sunlight.

He quickly looked away with an "Oh." Then he mumbled, "Uh, my dad wants me," and hurried to the far side of the pod.

Sky, hands on her hips, gave him the evil eye. "Jeesh!" She searched my face to see if I was upset. I wasn't. Not really. I'd seen reactions like his too many times.

I just tapped, **"No time to waste on turd boys!"**

"Ha!" She grinned wickedly and added, "Turd boys *are* waste." And then we started laughing so hard I got the hiccups.

As our capsule started the downward descent, Miss Gertie turned our view into an aerial map, showing us the different sections of London. That was a very cool way to think of the city, the way a bird saw it! That gull soared by again, which had me wondering how high birds could fly, and could smaller birds, like blue jays, fly as high as gulls? Then I was thinking how I was seeing London in a way folks like Shakespeare never had. Or Charles Dickens—I'd read *A Christmas Carol* last, you guessed it, Christmas. I tried to conjure up horse and buggies, cobblestone streets, candlelit streetlamps, characters like Jacob Marley and Bob Cratchit dashing through the city. Yikes, it would have been impossible to use a wheelchair on cobblestone streets. Still, I loved that I could sense the ancientness, the history of the city, from my bird's-eye view. And suddenly I was imagining Peter Pan flying through Wendy's opened window. Where would that have been on this air map?

I asked Miss Gertie, who said, "'Second to the right, and straight on till morning.'" She cocked her head and announced saucily, "Playing Wendy was one of my very first roles when I was a teenager! I remember the entire play!" Sky and I gaped as she then told us that Wendy's house was based on J. M. Barrie's own, not far from Kensington Palace.

I tapped, **"Second palace to the right!"** and Miss Gertie's laugh rang out.

This had us tumbling through our favorite British book characters.

"Robinson Crusoe," Sky said dreamily.

I nodded; he'd gotten shipwrecked on an island for like a million years.

"And David Copperfield and Sherlock Holmes and James Bond!" I tapped. My dad looooved James Bond.

Sky grinned. "Winnie the Pooh and Paddington Bear!"

"Willie Wonka and Harry Potter!"

"Matilda and Robin Hood!"

Mrs. V reminded us not to forget King Arthur or Alice in Wonderland.

The sweetest look came over Miss Gertie's face. "It seems so long ago, but so many of those characters—except for this Harry Potter fellow, who is he?—were a deeply important part of my life when I was a little girl. I can hardly express how thrilling it is to be back here visiting the land of my childhood book friends with my new friends."

She didn't have to express it, because I understood—I also felt really, really happy to be in the place where so many characters I'd read about had been created.

CHAPTER 25

By the time we got back to our hotel, I was so sleepy Mrs. V had to give me a wake-up shake . . . while she was brushing my teeth! Of course, once I spied a tiny beautifully wrapped package on each of our pillows, I woke right back up. Then nearly groaned when Mrs. V and Miss Gertie unwrapped theirs—each contained a chocolate truffle. But ohhhh! Mrs. V opened mine for me, and it wasn't chocolate at all! It was a twirl of pink meringue. Had Mom told the hotel about my chocolate thing, or was it the television station? I wasn't sure, so in my head, I thanked them both as I shared mine with Sky

and let the sugary air that was a meringue melt in my mouth. Then boom, fell asleep.

We woke up bananapants early on Thursday (thank you, jet lag). After a morning wash-up (the bathroom had special racks that kept your towels toasty warm, so we totally felt like royalty), Miss Gertie suggested ordering something called "bangers," which were like really fat sausages, and baked beans for breakfast. She'd just picked up the hotel phone to call for room service when a jazzy song from some old musical sang out from her own phone. She answered hesitantly with a "Good morning," then echoed that immediately with a much cheerier "Good morning to *you!*" She chatted away as Mrs. V got me dressed in a pink scoop-necked blouse, white jeans, and my new white Vans that Mom had gotten special for the trip. I reached toward my little jewelry bag on the bedside table, and Mrs. V knew exactly what I wanted: earrings.

"Silver hoops," I typed.

"Ooh, I have silver hoops," Sky exclaimed. "I'll wear mine, too."

We were admiring how hoop-fabulous we looked when we heard Miss Gertie say, "Wonderful! We'll meet you in the lobby in an hour." We turned to her expectantly.

"My niece, nephew, and great-nephew, Graham, are apparently so eager to see me that they refuse to wait until the weekend," she announced. "They've offered to pop over to the hotel and treat us to breakfast in about an hour."

Before we could react, Sky's phone rang out. I loved her ringtone—it's one of my favorite Double Trouble songs. If you happen to live under a rock, let me tell you that Double Trouble, in my humble opinion, is going to be the biggest band in the world! They were British as well! What was up with all the best boy bands coming from England? And Sky was into them too? I knew I liked this girl.

And now Sky was crying out, "Oliver! Yes, yes, we landed yesterday. . . . Today? . . . Really? . . . Can you really? Cool! Wait, WHAT? For REAL? Oh wow . . . Okay, let me coordinate and I'll call you back in a few. . . . Yeah, can't wait to see you, either."

Was I dying to know what the heck was going on? Heck yeah!

And suddenly plans for today were being planned and replanned and planned again. Sky's brother, who had an internship at Shakespeare's Globe Theatre, had unexpectedly been given the morning off; he just had to be back at work before the afternoon's performance. And he wanted to hang out with his sister. And, apparently, me.

They hadn't seen each other since Christmas! I couldn't imagine not seeing my family for over six months. No wonder Sky sounded so excited.

And that wasn't all. Because he worked at the Globe, he was able to snag some free last-minute tickets for all four of us for the afternoon performance of *Romeo and Juliet*! *Romeo and Juliet*, which I chose to read for an English paper last fall (and got an A++ on it—not bragging, just stating facts). Did we want to go? Of course we did!

Miss Gertie decided it would be more fun for Sky and me to go do some exploring with Oliver instead of breakfast with her relatives. Then she insisted that Mrs. V join her instead. When Mrs. V protested, not wanting to be in the way and unsure about having me off on my own with Sky, Miss Gertie shook her head firmly. "I need you! They can't pepper me with eight thousand questions if you're with me! They'll mean well, but they can be a nosy bunch!"

And so it was settled. Sky and I chose the British Museum and the Wallace Collection as our morning adventure. Not only because they were high on our Gotta Do list, but both required a lot of walking, and we didn't want Miss Gertie to feel she had to keep up.

Oliver lived on the opposite side of London. Luckily, the British Museum was right in between us both. And believe it or not, Mrs. V said she was quite comfortable with Sky and me taking a cab to meet him there. This was after Sky convinced her that she could roll me in and out of the cab no problem, declaring she'd spent all summer working on a horse farm, and I weighed about a tenth as much as a horse, and did Mrs. V have any idea how heavy manure was to shovel? Probably because she didn't want to get into a manure conversation, Mrs. V caved. Yes! We would meet back at the hotel at one o'clock, so we could be at the Globe by two. It was a perfect plan.

CHAPTER 26

There we were, me and Sky, all alone in the big city, cue the music! Okay, so we were actually all alone on the big sidewalk. (London sidewalks are wiiiiiide; great for wheelchairs!) We had double-checked that Elvira was charged and that Sky's cell phone was charging, gobbled down some oatmeal, made sure that Mrs. V and I had Sky's number, that I had a snack in case I got hungry later. I even went to the bathroom twice to be sure I'd be good for the next few hours, and here we were, hailing a cab like we were Londoners.

Yesterday, Miss Gertie had asked the bellhop to get us a cab, but this morning he was busy helping someone who had, like, forty pieces of luggage. Sky and I wanted to go Go GO! so we were getting a cab ourselves.

I was looking everywhere at once—wow, was it busy! The sidewalk was packed with people heading to . . . who knows, it looked like everywhere. Loads of folks carried umbrellas, even though we'd lucked out with another sunny day. Cars lined up along the curb for as far as we could see. The park across the street, which looked lush—probably because there was usually so much rain here—was full of dog walkers. Though, ha-ha, a few people looked like their dogs were walking them. A woman waltzed by us, holding the leashes of four identical, stocky little pups, French bulldogs I think they're called. They huffed and snorted as they trotted by, giving my wheels and Sky's sneakers a good snortle-sniff along the way.

"They should rename that breed Snortles," I typed, watching them waddle down the street.

"Totally!" she agreed, then shouted, "Oh, there's a cab!" She dashed to the curb and flung her arm out as if she'd done it a million times, and, yep, that big black cab pulled right over alongside one of the parked cars.

The driver hopped out and met us at the curb. "G'day, m'ladies," he greeted us. His accent was much thicker than Miss Gertie's. He had a cheery grin, his cheeks were pink, and he looked delighted to see us. Even though it was summer, he wore a linen jacket the exact color of my shirt, and a bow tie. I'd never actually seen a real live person wear one of those before!

"Good morning," Sky said back.

"Here, let me assist." He took the handlebars of my chair, guided me right between the two parked cars, opened the back door to his cab, and pulled down a short ramp, all in one fell swoop. "And where might you young ladies be off to on this fine morning?" the cab driver asked as he lined the wheels of my chair up with the ramp.

"Thank you. We're going to the British Museum, which is on—" Sky reached into the back pocket of her jean shorts for her phone. She inhaled sharply. Checked the front pockets. "Dang it! Melody, I think I left my phone on the floor, charging!" She gave a groan. "Sir, could you wait literally thirty seconds? I just have to run up to our room and get my phone."

The driver waved her off with a "Not to worry. I'll have your friend Melody here secured and ready to go by the time you've returned, and then *we'll* be ready to go in two shakes of a lamb's tail."

"Thank you, thank you so much," Sky said in a rush, then spun around and ran for those massive wooden doors.

"I'm ever so pleased to make your acquaintance, m'lady," the driver said to me, tipping a make-believe hat. I grinned. "I'm Theodore Beasley," he continued, pushing my wheelchair up the ramp with ease. "But my friends call me Teddy. I'd be honored if you'd do the same."

Would he be surprised by Elvira? I wondered. I decided to find out. **"Pleased to meet you, Teddy!"** I typed.

He attached some brackets to the back wheels of my chair, gave them a tug, and sat in the seat across from me. "Well, isn't that a marvel of a computer you have there, love."

"It is! It's the best gift I ever got!"

Teddy was nodding in agreement when there was a sharp tap on the window. He jumped up, whacked his head on the roof, let out an "ouch," and then, "Blimey, a bobby." He hopped out of the cab. Through the door, I saw a uniform, and, wriggling down a little more, I saw that it was a police officer. They called them "bobby" here? That was a question for later. The question for now was, why was he now rapping the roof of the cab, gesticulating wildly, then waving as if shooing us away?

"But sir, I'm waiting for this young lady's friend; she'll be here in a jiff," Teddy was saying.

"I don't care if you're waiting for the prime minister himself! There's no double-parking in this zone. You'll have to move. Now."

"But . . ."

The police officer took off his hat, a really high black one, with a massive metal emblem on it (wow, the British like their high hats!), wiped his brow, and said in the *I'm not saying this again* tone of voice that my teachers use, "You can move your cab or get a bleedin' ticket. But you'll move even if you get a ticket." He didn't understand! I needed Sky. I gave a grunt. The bobby ignored me.

Teddy looked at me in dismay. "A thousand apologies, m'lady. Would you mind if we circled the block? Your friend will be out by then."

I didn't want Teddy to get a ticket. And we'd have to move anyway. So I nodded reluctantly—there was nothing else to do. He checked my brackets one last time, climbed into the front of the cab, and pulled away. The grump of a police officer was already banging on the top of another car that was double-parked.

"We'll be round the block in two shakes," Teddy assured me from the front. Two shakes of a lamb's tail— now I got it: fast! Except two shakes wasn't how we got around the block. The street to turn on was closed off! And there was so. Much. Traffic. Dad thinks traffic's bad at home, but this was a sea of cars. I did get to look at shop windows, where I saw a shirt perfect for Sky. And a bakery that—ooh, ooh!—had scones that I really wanted to try, and slices of so, so, soooo many different types of cakes that I couldn't count them fast enough. A couple bounced out of that shop with a slice of cake on a plate, as if they'd gotten a slice of pizza. Mrs. V definitely had to bring us there.

As we inched along, my new friend Teddy chatted away. He'd been widowed in "aught-eight," which I deciphered to mean 2008, so three years ago. And he was retired, but drove a cab to make "a bit of pin money," and he liked to "chat people up," which I think meant "extra money" and "talking to people." He had a "wee grandbaby" who lived fifty kilometers away, but that was just a "nip on the train." I felt I was learning a whole new language! I started to rethink my choice if one day I invented a way for Elvira to speak in any voice I chose. Sorry, Beyoncé, but I needed a British accent!

We made it around the first turn at last. But right before the next one, we slowed to a complete stop. Two double-decker buses had run too close to each other, and their side mirrors hit. The drivers were in the middle of the street, yelling at each other. Teddy apologized as if it were all his fault.

"Just a few more turns and we'll be back at the hotel, don't you worry!" he assured me. At first I *had* been a little worried, having to leave the hotel like that, but Teddy was being so reassuring that my panic subsided. To tell the truth, I felt pretty fancy, sitting there in a cab all by myself, as if I were all that. Even if it was just for a

few minutes! Plus, I spied that bookstore—Hatchards—
Miss Gertie had mentioned. Two British flags flew above
the entry, and there was a fancy-schmancy wooden shield
with a lion on one side and a unicorn on the other
guarding the doors.

"That's the seal of the royal family, m'lady," Teddy
told me proudly. "Hatchards has been in business since
the late 1700s. It's where the royal family gets many of
their books. Queen Elizabeth herself gave it a seal of
approval!"

Miss Gertie will be happy to know it's this close, I thought.
As if he'd read my mind, Teddy asked about my visit. I
told him about the surprise trip, and when he heard that
I was with Miss Gertie, a British actress from back in the
day who now lived in the States, he gave a loud gasp.

"Would you mind terribly if I inquired as to Miss
Gertie's last name?"

"It's Gilson."

"You don't say!" But I did just say! But I didn't say that
to Teddy. Before I could respond, he went on. "Ohhh,
did I ever fancy Miss Gilson when I was at university. She
was studying theater in her final year as I was starting my
first. Mind you, half the lads fancied Gertie. She didn't
know me from a can of beans, but she always said hello
as we passed in the halls. The very first play I ever saw
was because Gertie Gilson was in it." He said this in such

a rush I wondered how he didn't keel over from lack of oxygen. "Fancied" must be old-timey for "had a crush on," and I felt so glad that this sweet man had a crush on Miss Gertie!

By now, several "bobbies" were gathered around the bus drivers. They all must practice the shoo-wave in bobby school, because they were shooing the buses away in unison, until we finally started moving.

"I won't be charging you for this," Teddy said out of the blue. Which made me realize, we'd been gone for ages! Sky must be mega-worried. Ohhh, I hope she didn't tell Mrs. V! I quickly called Sky's number on Elvira.

"Melody! Oh my GOSH. Are you okay? Where are you—"

I interrupted her as fast as I could so she'd stop panicking. **"I'm fine. Police made us move. Nearly back at hotel."**

"Melody! I was scared you'd been kidnapped! I just finished telling a police officer—I didn't want to freak out Mrs. V or Aunt Gertie yet, but I was about to go back to the room—" And at that moment, we pulled up to the hotel. To a blur.

Sky was jumping and shouting and waving.

A red-faced bobby was running toward us.

Then a second.

The first bobby swung open my door.

The second whacked at Teddy's window.

The first leaned in and cried out, "You!" to me.

Then he leaned into the passenger-side window and cried out, "You!" to Teddy. The second bobby looked completely confused.

Sky scrambled into the back of the cab and practically jumped on me in a hug.

And there was explaining and re-explaining and they were finally convinced I was fine (maybe because I told them I was fine about forty thousand times). Teddy explained to the second bobby how the first bobby was the one who'd made him drive off and leave Sky behind and there was traffic, and, and, and then bobby number two started telling off bobby number one for being so thoughtless and hadn't he seen I was in a wheelchair, and OMG. Yeah, there was drama! Finally, Sky and I just started laughing, because, during all this, a *third* bobby came up to stuffily inform us . . . that we were double-parked!

Fortunately, getting to the British Museum really did only take two shakes of a lamb's tail—no traffic in that direction. Sky earned a "my friends call me Teddy" as well, but he called her Miss Sky instead of m'lady. She apologized for telling bobby #2 about the situation, but what if I'd been kidnapped? Teddy said she'd done exactly the right thing. Then he gave us some pointers on his favorite "bits" in the museum and said the Wallace Collection was his favorite in all of London; he hoped we'd love it too. When he asked if we were going to take in a show (which I think meant go see a play at the theater?), we told him about how we were all going to the Globe in the afternoon.

He went quiet for a moment, then, clearing his voice a few times, said, "You'll never catch a cab at that time of day. All the public schools will be letting out, and the place is mad with kids being picked up. Tell you what, I'll plan to be right up front of the Marlington at one o'clock sharp—*not* double-parked, mind you—and drive you all over myself." He let out a deep chortling laugh.

"Deal!" Sky agreed.

"Deal," I tapped as well. **"Thank you!"** Teddy swung up to the museum, swung me out of the cab, and with a "Cheers," gave a salute and a promise to see us at one.

CHAPTER 27

Oliver looked just like his sister—a sprinkle of freckles, banana-brown eyes, reddish-brown hair that was just the right length, and a huge smile of slightly crooked teeth. Sky ran over to where he was waiting by the main stairway into the museum and threw her arms around him. He swung her around, then pulled away to look at her. He poked at the streaks in her hair.

"Your hair—Mom didn't kill you?"

She laughed. "Nah. I said I wanted to get a cartilage piercing at first, and she liked this idea a *lot* better."

Oliver shook his head, grinning. "Aren't you the

clever one!" Then he turned to me. "And you must be the famous Melody!"

"Infamous is more like it," Sky quipped. "She nearly caused a national security incident back at the hotel!"

"I know how to make an entrance," I joked.

"Ah, someone who can give it back to my sister. I like you already," Oliver said, pushing his hair behind his ears, fake-punching his sister in the shoulder.

Sky was bouncing up and down on her toes. "I'm psyched that you're free this morning!"

"I'm psyched you found your way to London, kiddo. Oh, Mom and Dad called from Afghanistan this morning. They said it's totally chaotic and completely disorganized over there. Guess that's why they're there."

"Did they give a better idea of how long they'd be away this time?" I detected a hint of sadness in Sky's voice.

Oliver gave a little shrug. Sky glanced at me and sighed. I could tell she really missed her parents. I was so lucky that I had all my family around me all the time. I hoped Penny wasn't feeling as sad about me being gone as Sky clearly was about her parents.

Sky tossed her red-streaked head. "One day I'll travel around the world just like they do. And make a difference too." She straightened her shoulders and gripped the handles of my wheelchair. "Now, let's see the parts of the world in this museum!" Then she let out a wistful laugh. "Well, the parts of the world I haven't seen. Sometimes I feel like I see more of the world than I do . . . of my parents." I reached up and brushed her hand.

Sky didn't know how right she was about the British Museum. It seemed to have something from everywhere, and the way it was set up, by different cultures, felt like a micro world tour. There were sooo many ancient sculptures, lots over 2,500 years old. Literally more than two hundred times older than me! It was hard to get my head around that much time, and the fact that all these things had survived that long. Most of the sculptures, though, had a hand or leg or even a head missing. Which made me sad for them. Which then made me kind of chuckle—here I was, empathizing with statues!

One famous statue was from Easter Island (I'd have to look up where that was), and for some reason I could feel a power radiating from it. When we got to the Chinese wing, I couldn't believe all the intricate carved horses and camels and dragons and mythical creatures that had been made just to get packed into someone's tomb. They were literally called tomb guardians! And there were mummies, too, yep, REAL mummies. Like, unwrapped!! There were ancient snake carvings from Mexico, and while snakes kind of give me the willies, there was one bright blue double-headed one I couldn't stop staring at. Good thing Oliver knew the highlights, as there was almost too much to look at. From Scotland to Africa to Micronesia, yeah, it really was like a mini gathering of the ancient world.

I nudged Sky, then tapped, **"Imagine if the people who made these things all came to life, right now!"**

Sky turned in a circle, a strange look on her face, almost like it could actually happen.

Oliver swiveled around, eyebrows raised. "I want to think about that. It'd be a great idea for a book."

"Are you studying writing in college?"

"It's not my focus, but I always take one writing course a semester, 'cause I always have some story in my head that wants to get out." He gave me a fake-annoyed look. "Now you've given me another one!"

"You're welcome!"

"I've saved one of the most amazing pieces for last," Oliver told us as we left the Middle Eastern galleries and headed to the Egyptian sculpture gallery. He wasn't the only one who thought it was amazing—it seemed like half the people in the museum were stuffed into that room. Oliver took charge of my wheelchair and excuse-me, excuse-me, excuse-me'd right to the front. Where, sitting in a carefully lit glass case, was . . . the Rosetta Stone.

Right there, in front of me. Covered with carvings of pale, delicate hieroglyphs, and Egyptian and Greek letters. How did I not know it was here? I was obsessed with hieroglyphics when I was younger. I remember wishing so much that I could write and draw, because it would be so cool to write secret messages using hieroglyphics. The Rosetta Stone was the key that helped people understand what the hieroglyphics actually said. Until then, nothing seemed to exist that explained their meaning. The Rosetta Stone was like, an Elvira! All those carvings on sarcophaguses and walls, and notes on mummies, were clearly telling stories, but for thousands of years, they were a mystery. And here it was, the key. How wild was that? The stone was very worn in places; I would be too if I was two thousand years old.

"It's so valuable that during World War I, it was hidden in a railway tunnel so if the city were bombed, it would be safe," Oliver was telling us. And now I was officially re-obsessed with hieroglyphics.

"I really want to touch it," Sky admitted. "Guess that's why there's a shatter-proof case around it!"

"They knew you were coming, ha-ha," I tapped.

Oliver tipped his head to one side, watching us. "It's like you two have known each other for forever," he said. "Melody, I'm so glad you and my sister are friends. I had it so much easier—my parents traveled a lot less when I was little. Sky was yanked all over the place."

Huh? Sky needed *me*? I was the one who'd always wanted a friend like Sky. It had never occurred to me that someone like Sky could need a friend like me.

CHAPTER 28

Have you ever thought about what it could really feel like to be a knight in armor? I have. I know, bizarre. But from the first time I ever saw a picture of one, I think reading Robin Hood or King Arthur stories, I'd been curious. Was armor heavy? Was it uncomfortable? How hard was it to move your body? And how the heck did you run in it? Maybe because I have almost no control over how my body works, it got me wondering. Anyway! As soon as I'd read that the Wallace Collection had rooms full of all kinds of armor, I had to go.

Oliver brought us to the tube, which was a British version of a subway, so we could get there super fast.

The tube was so easy! Elevators brought us right to the platforms, and the subway train came right to the edge of the platforms, so I could roll right on. And there was an area on every car that was wide enough for a wheelchair without blocking other people, which I'm always worried I'm doing. Go tube!

We then walked down a tree-lined street past lots of very fancy-looking homes, until Oliver stopped in front of, well, a very, VERY fancy one with columns and everything. Huh? But as Oliver announced, "We're here! The Wallace Collection! After you." Sky zipped right in, so I pressed the forward button on my chair and zipped in as well. Sky paid the entrance fee with our British pounds (which, sorry, America, are way more interesting-looking than dollars!), telling her brother this was our treat.

We went straight to the floor where they had the armor, and *I* was floored! It was like stepping into an ancient closet of history and mystery. We circled around display after display of the armor—from all around the world—that the warriors and their horses wore in battle. Mannequins of knights, cloaked in iron, loomed everywhere, giving off Touch-Us-and-Off-with-Your-Head vibes. Just looking at some of them was scary—especially the ones with the fully enclosed head helmets, the only openings being slits to see from. Yikes. There were even full-size knights on full-size horses, some rearing. The thought, *What if this all suddenly came to life?* struck me again. We would be . . . dead meat! Ha ha ha.

I couldn't get over how thick the armor was. Some was made of overlapping metal plates, and others were made of what looked kinda like knitted wires. How did anyone fight in that? Or run? And what about their horses? How did *they* run in armor? I felt instantly sorry for the horses of five hundred years ago. And the foot coverings, holy moly! Some had a long, evil-looking spike coming out from the tip. So you could stab people with your foot! Who thought of this kind of stuff?! I tried to imagine those on me—with my mind-of-their-own legs, everyone would be in danger!

Some of the armor made no sense. Fancy feathers puffed up like plumes from the tops of some helmets. It seemed to me that that would for sure make you an easy target for the enemy. And a lot of the armor was covered with intricate patterns; the horses' armor too. A lot of work just to go off to a war if you asked me!

I pointed this out to Sky. **"Think they had armor fashion shows back in the Renaissance?"**

"Ha! Imagine a line of knights on a catwalk!" Sky joked.

Then I saw a plaque that said most full-body armor weighed between forty and fifty pounds. I did a quick calculation—that would be like trying to fight a battle with Penny hanging on my back. Medieval dudes must have been super fit. I was betting all the soldiers were men back then—unless some clever girl disguised herself so she could fight with the guys. I'm pretty bold, but nah, I wouldn't volunteer for battle!

Some armor even had what looked like skirts! Sky read one of the informational displays. "They needed to be able to get on their horses in a hurry." I wheeled closer. The skirt-looking bottom part of some of the armor looked shingled, almost movable. Huh. Well, that made sense. Which then led my brain to: How did they even *make* such thick, heavy, complicated armor way back then? Power tools hadn't been invented. Power hadn't even been invented. I gotta give them their props!

Sky kept reading. "The bottom part slid up for easy riding of the horse. And in case they had to poop!" As we both cracked up, we could tell Oliver was trying hard not to laugh as well.

"Hey, guys, there's a video of how they actually forged the armor. Wanna watch?" he asked. Sky and I looked at each other. Of course we did! The takeaway? You had to be big and brawny just to make the armor that you had to be big and brawny to wear! And not be afraid of fire—armor was made of chunks of searing hot metal welded together!

As we discussed how armor making was not in our futures, Oliver let out an "Oh, SHOOT!"

"What's wrong?" Sky asked in alarm.

He grimaced. "It's just that there are so many other floors to see, but we have to leave in a minute and get back to your hotel." Oh, right, the play! As we headed out, though, we spied the gift shop. We had to go in. Had to.

Sky gave her most conniving grin. "You said one minute. We can be in and out in one minute, right, Melody?"

"Please?" I added. I was imagining a miniature suit of armor for one of Penny's naked Barbies.

"'Cause I'm feeling generous, I'll give you two. We're not that far from the hotel, actually." He waved us in, saying he needed to check his texts.

"I dub thee a great guy," I tapped, and rolled after Sky.

CHAPTER 29

The gift shop was more for adults than kids—scarves based on paintings in the museum's collection, boxes of cards, pens made of feathers, tea sets made of something called bone china. Um, huh? And for some random reason, lots of little jars of jam. I was thinking we weren't going to need even one minute here when I saw them toward the back. Helmets. And shields. And tiny catapults.

Sky catapulted herself right over there. By the time I wove around a display of scarves, she'd already fitted a plastic helmet over her head. She held another in her right hand, and two shields in her left. I grinned wildly. I didn't have time to type anything because she propped one shield up against my chest and stuck the helmet over my head. At that I gave a grunt—it was tight!

Sky wedged one of those feather pens between my thumb and first finger.

"En garde!" she exclaimed, posing like Lancelot. Then she play-attacked my feather pen with another feather pen, and I was dying. My arm swung wildly back at her, and somehow my hand behaved and held on to the feather pen. Sky looked so silly in her helmet—it was bronze-colored, with a super-pointy nose and lots of holes to breathe through. I wished I could take a picture of her; I wished I could tell her to take a selfie; but I was too busy trying not to be killed. Almost doubled-up laughing, I swung out and miraculously knocked Sky's feather from her hand.

"I am perished!" she cried out, then fell to the ground in a swoon.

"Ahem."

We both looked up (which, by the way, was NOT easy to do with a helmet on, even a plastic one!). A very proper-looking woman was standing over us, arms folded, eyebrows raised, lips pursed. Even the pearl necklace around her neck looked annoyed. Uh-oh. Busted!

Sky scrambled up. "Oh my gosh, we're so, so sorry! We got carried away—"

But before Sky could finish her apology, the woman let out a tinkling laugh.

"I haven't seen anyone have such a giggle here for eons." She paused. "I'm a patron of the museum, and I'm always looking for ways to coax younger people to come visit. And you've confirmed my suspicions—more fun items at the gift shop."

By this time I'd shaken the feather from my hand and could type again. **"We really are very sorry! We'll pay for these!"**

Now the woman looked aghast. Oh boy, we were in mega trouble for sure! Was she going to call the bobbies? But no—the opposite.

"Oh, my dear girls, I wouldn't hear of it! You've added a spark to my day; I insist you take them all, as my gift."

"But—" Sky started to protest.

"Not another word. We'll consider it market research." She stroked her pearls, winked, and told us she'd get us a bag "for your loot."

"Uh, what the heck are you guys doing?" There was Oliver, mouth open, a hand on his head. Sky quickly explained. "Birds of a feather, that's what you two are," he said. "C'mon, we have to get going!"

Sky yanked her helmet off and tucked it under her arm. But when Oliver went to remove mine, it didn't budge. He gave a little tug. Nothing. A harder tug. Still nothing. He and Sky glanced at each other.

"Uh, Melody, I think it's stuck around your chin," Sky said.

Oliver asked, "Do you think you can handle me pulling harder?" I nodded. He shimmied both sets of fingers under the bottom of the helmet and did a sort of jiggle-pull upward. The front rose up an inch, just enough so that my head bobbled. Now the eye slits were at my forehead, and I couldn't see! I grunted, and grunted again.

"It's okay, I'm sure this has happened before!" Oliver assured me, but I could hear a sliver of nervousness in his voice. When he jiggle-pulled it once more, however, the helmet stayed exactly where it was. I wasn't panicking. I wasn't panicking. Okay, I was starting to panic a little. How many people in London knew how to undo knights' helmets, even plastic ones? Probably not many. And Miss Gertie was going to be so disappointed if we missed *Romeo and Juliet*!

One leg started kicking. To keep myself calm, I tried to think of something that would be worse. Being stuck with a whole suit of armor on and having to pee! That would be worse! I started snort-laughing, but through the helmet it must have sounded different, because Oliver whispered way too loud, "Sky, I think she's crying!"

"Melody, we're right here! And really, this probably happens all the time."

Then I felt taps all over my head—or actually, on the

helmet over my head. "I'm not feeling any weak spots." Oliver was still loud-whispering, and now his whispering was definitely sounding panicky.

Hello, I can hear you, I wished I could say. Or type! But I couldn't see to type, and I couldn't use Elvira to tell them I couldn't see. How do these things always happen to me?

Then Sky let out a triumphant cry. I had no idea what she was doing, but suddenly I smelled what seemed like a field's worth of lavender.

"Hang on, Melody. I'm going to rub lotion around your chin. Maybe that'll help." The smell got stronger as Sky slathered the lotion around.

"Okay, now try again," she told her brother. He pulled the helmet back down, then rocked it back and forth, back and forth, slowly lifting at the same time. And it started to move! And then it was off! We gaped at each other, panting. Sky and Oliver looked so upset I had to assure them I was totally fine. And better-smelling than when we got here.

"Looks like we're buying something after all," Sky said at last, holding out a bottle of lotion that said MADE WITH PURE ENGLISH LAVENDER. More of the same bottles were lined up on a table right behind her.

"I'll bring the rest home to my mom."

"Saved by the lavender," Oliver observed, and we all laughed.

CHAPTER 30

I now know what a whirlwind is. It is:

—racing back to the hotel . . .

—Oliver immediately racing after the cab
because we rushed out without our bag of
"loot," as the Patron Lady called it . . .

—Oliver being gushed over by Miss Gertie
(apparently he had grown a foot since she'd
last seen him at age ten) . . .

—me being fed the world's quickest lunch ever
(clever Mrs. V had ordered ahead so it was
waiting for us when we returned) . . .

—Miss Gertie gushing about her visit with her
  relatives . . .
—changing into dresses for me and Sky . . .
—trip to the bathroom (Mrs. V wondering why I
  smelled so nice) . . .
—back to the lobby of the hotel, and Sky triple-
  checking she had her phone, even though it
  was IN HER HAND . . .

And PHEW . . . there was Teddy, not double-parked
but in the hotel's circular drive, with the back passen-
ger door already swung open. I noticed how he stood
straighter, shoulders back, as we came out the door, and
straighter still when he saw Miss Gertie. And when she
reached the door, he *bowed*! He literally bowed! We said
our hellos and hello, m'ladies and nice-to-meet-yous,
then Teddy popped open that little ramp and wheeled
me in. With a flourish, he held out a hand to help Mrs.
V, then Sky, then Miss Gertie, into the cab. When he let
go of Miss Gertie's hand, his cheeks were tinged even
pinker than usual. He moved aside to let Oliver plop
himself in the jump seat beside me.

"To the Globe!" Teddy declared, and gently closed
the door. Hmm. I had to get him and Miss Gertie talking! But as we sped through the streets—well, sped,
slowed down, sped, slowed down . . . really, London had

major traffic issues (was it like this in all big cities?)—Sky struck up a conversation instead.

"Melody has read all of Shakespeare's plays," she told her brother. When Oliver looked at me in surprise, she added, "Yep, every one!"

I grinned in agreement. Lots of kids at school think Shakespeare is hard, but it's just old. The folks who lived in England in the 1500s simply spoke a different variation of English—the old-school, historically cool version. And I mean *really* old-school! Shakespeare wrote *Romeo and Juliet* somewhere around 1595! And here I was, going to see it live!

"Well, that's mighty impressive." Oliver pushed his hair behind his ears. "You might want to get a summer job here—it's for sure the best one I've *ever* had! I get to see the shows for free!"

I was wondering what sort of job I could do at a theater company—maybe write programs?—when Sky leaned forward to tell me, "You know, most of the seating there is standing room only."

"Huh?" I tapped.

She cracked up. "*Everybody* stands! There are no chairs!"

"Betcha I get to sit!" I tapped, sticking my tongue out.

Miss Gertie thought that was very funny. I loved seeing how bright and full of energy she was since we'd arrived in London. Right now, she was eyeing our cabdriver, a quizzical look on her face. So I made a decision. I tapped my volume to high.

"Mr. Teddy! Thank you for picking us up. And meeting Mrs. V and Miss Gertie."

"What-what? Entirely my pleasure, m'lady!" Then he turned to take a quick glance at Miss Gertie, who was wearing the very same hat she'd worn at Channel 12. "And if you don't mind me saying so, Miss Gilson, it's a tremendous honor to have you in my cab."

"Well, aren't you kind," Miss Gertie said demurely.

"We weren't in the same year, but we were at university together in the 1960s."

"Oh, you were at Exeter as well, then?"

"I was indeed. Studied music. Trumpet, mostly, but bagpipes were a close second; me ma loved them so."

"Ah, I do adore the bagpipes. My study was drama. It was all I could think about, day and night. I'd sneak away to London any chance I got to see a play. One could afford them those days!"

Teddy belly-laughed. "I hope it pleases you to know that I snuck out of many a study group to see plays you were in." He gulped, then added, "My very first West End play . . . was to watch you in *Peter Pan*!"

"Glory be! Well, I hope I put on a worthy performance and didn't cost you a grade," Gertie said, her own cheeks now pink.

"It was brilliant!" Teddy paused, then said, his tone slightly wistful, "Ah, there she is, up ahead, the Globe."

I remember looking up info on the Globe Theatre when I'd read *Romeo and Juliet.* Most people had to stand back then as well. It was opened in 1599, and the first play performed there was *Julius Caesar.* Then it burned down, I think, and got rebuilt . . . and then . . . Hmm, I forget. So I asked Oliver.

"Exactly right, Melody. Or, ha-ha, should I call you m'lady too? This current Globe opened in 1997. Its pillars," he explained with gusto, "are made from two oak trees that are painted to look like marble. And it's the only building in London allowed to have a thatched roof."

"Why's that?" Sky wanted to know.

"The Great Fire in 1666—half the city turned into ashes. So no more thatched roofs! Except, of course, here."

Oliver was in tour guide mode for sure. And he was also a mind reader, like his sister, because he answered my next question before I even asked it.

"And here's the coolest thing I know!" he said, knee bouncing with excitement. "Since almost no one could read back then, you couldn't really put up flyers or advertise plays in newspapers. So the theater had a flag system that let people know the type of play running that night. Black flags were for a tragedy, white flags meant a comedy, and red flags were for historical pieces."

"So smart!" I typed. We were just pulling up to the theater, and I couldn't help looking to the top, to see if there was a flag.

There wasn't, but I was cheesing like mad anyway. So much of my life has been made of dreams and wishes. To think I might actually be able to *be* in a place I'd only read about or seen in old movies was like being able to wake up and touch one of those dreams.

CHAPTER 31

I'm not sure if Teddy was a master at teleportation (or knew someone from *Doctor Who*—yeah, I was totally into that show, and so was Sky! I swear if I saw David Tennant walking down the street, I'd fall out of my wheelchair!). But either we were quicker getting ready than we thought, or we'd misjudged the time, but we arrived super early!

Oliver thought this was fabulous. "Now I can introduce you to Mr. Hammond. He's the director!" He bolted out of the cab, asking Teddy, "How many quid?" Quid? Then I saw him pulling out his wallet. Money, was that what quid was? Sky was unlocking my wheels as Teddy made his way around the car to first help the others out, then me.

"I'll swing back round once the play is through," he offered. "It'll be hard to get a taxi when it's over, and I don't want you having to wait in a queue."

"Are you sure, Teddy?" Miss Gertie asked.

"Little would please me more," he said, beaming.

From the outside, the Globe Theatre didn't look like it had in the 1600s, but the bricks were worn, the crowds were thick, and anticipation was in the air.

As Oliver led us past a very modern-looking lobby and concession area, I felt a tinge of disappointment. . . . This was it? But then he swung open a pair of double doors, and inside, it was almost like we had been propelled into the past. I could imagine what it must have been like, before computers or television, and when most people couldn't read, so books weren't a thing either. People must have been so excited to come here, crowding into a building where actors were ready to entertain them with stories of bravery and romance. I mean, I was excited, and I had all kinds of entertainment at my thumb-tip!

Miss Gertie placed her hand over her heart as we entered. I'd been wondering how she would feel coming here, having been away from the stage for so long. But her movement, and her watering eyes, let me know exactly. A little flame of happiness flickered inside me as well.

"Is Mr. Hammond around?" Oliver asked a young woman with a high ponytail and a clipboard, dressed all in black, even down to her ballet slippers. "I have someone very special with me who I think he'd want to meet." The woman tipped her head, ponytail swinging, thinking.

"Hmm, I just saw him backstage, fussing about Juliet's costume. I'll go fetch him." She swiveled, then gave a full-body wave to a tall, slender Black man walking across the stage. He too was dressed all in black, except for the coolest glasses I'd ever seen—bright orange! "Mr. Hammond! Can you spare a moment?"

Mr. Hammond glanced our way, gave a little jog, and hopped easily off the stage. He said hello to Oliver and looked us over curiously.

Oliver stepped forward. "I wouldn't bother you just before a show, but I'm with my great-aunt, who's visiting from—"

Oliver didn't have a chance to finish. "Is this . . . is this Miss Gilson? Gertie Gilson?" The director actually looked flustered. He looked from Oliver to Miss Gertie, then from one to the other again. Miss Gertie must have been used to this from earlier times, as she gave him her brightest smile, and the slightest nod, then held out a hand, almost regally. Mr. Hammond took it with both of his.

"Zounds, I wasn't expecting this! I'm a tremendous fan! When I was a boy, my own nan brought me to my first play on the West End. It was *A Christmas Carol*, and you were Mrs. Fezziwig. I was perhaps a bit too young for the play—I daresay it seemed rather dreary to me at times—but you lit up the stage. And because of you, I wanted to go to another play. Gave me the bug, one would say. And look at me—"

Then he stopped short as he realized he was still shaking her hand. "I haven't felt this flustered in ever so long. This is a marvelous—" He paused as his cell phone went off. "Please, excuse me for just one moment." He pulled the phone from his pocket, saw who it was, and turned away.

Oliver looked alarmed when Mr. Hammond turned back to us a few moments later, saying, "I'm afraid I must cut our greeting short. I'm in a bit of a pickle."

"Sir, can I help?" Oliver offered immediately.

"Not unless you can transform yourself into Juliet's mother." The director sighed. "Annabelle's flight from Edinburgh was delayed—they only just departed. She's going to miss her call. I told her last night she was cutting it close, but her mum is in hospital and Annabelle's understudy called in sick. . . . We have no one to play Lady Capulet!" Then he paused yet again, a strange expression crossing his face.

I wondered if he was thinking what I was thinking. Turns out, he was.

CHAPTER 32

It took a lot of convincing. There was a lot of Miss Gertie protesting, "I couldn't possibly!" and then more convincing, then more of Miss Gertie protesting, "But I haven't trod the boards in decades." But if a big-time Shakespeare's Globe director and I had the exact same thought, it must be a good one. So finally, I tapped my volume up as high as it would go.

"Miss Gertie. You told me how brave I was. And because I was, I got to meet you and I am so lucky! You are wonderful and kind and generous. And Miss G, you've got chops! People will remember this forever if you surprise them onstage."

I stopped for a moment to rest my thumb; I could tell everyone, but especially Miss Gertie, was watching me. **"You told me to tell you if there was anything you could ever do for me. I would like it to be this! Please, pretty please?"**

The director grinned at us both and raised his clutched hands up to his chin. "Please, pretty please?" he echoed in the sweetest voice. "And imagine the reviews! Guest star, Gertrude Gilson!"

"Well, if it's for the reviews, how can I say no?" Miss Gertie finally said, like a true professional (or at least how I imagined a true professional would answer). But then she added, with a toss of her head, "And how can I say no to Melody? If she summoned her courage, well, I can too. In fact, I feel I've been called back to London just for this moment! So, lay on, Macduff! I would be honored to play Lady Capulet this evening."

Miss Gertie was going to play Lady Capulet, Juliet's mother. How awesome was that?! The woman with the high ponytail whisked us backstage for a quick peek as she looked for the person in charge of costumes, sure there was one that would fit Miss Gertie. We stood off to one side, away from the commotion, and that was when Miss Gertie suddenly went pale. Mrs. V noticed instantly.

"Gertie, what is it? Are you feeling ill? Is it your head?"

"Oh, no, no, no. It's just that it's been forty years

since I was in *Romeo and Juliet*. I once knew those lines as well as my own name, but . . . forty years of memories is a lot to sift through. I do wish they'd hurry a bit with that script." We looked around; everyone looked very busy doing very important things and none of it involved bringing Miss Gertie a script. And Oliver had left to start his ushering duties; the audience was arriving.

I was about to tell Miss Gertie that someone would for sure bring one by, but as my thumb hovered over the keyboard, I suddenly realized: Elvira! That was how I'd read *Romeo and Juliet* in the first place. The play was sitting right in the memory (along with my A++ paper).

Seconds later, the play was up on my screen. I was so excited my right arm kept flinging out, making it hard to type anything more, but the flinging caught their attention. I grunted, and Sky squatted down to look at my screen.

"Melody has the play!" She jumped back up and clutched Miss Gertie's arm. "We can sneak in practice right here!"

Miss Gertie's face rosied right up. "Right, then. Melody, read me the lines."

"Me?"

Miss Gertie fixed her eye on me. "Why not you?"

Huh. Yeah. Why not me? I tried to stay calm, but the idea of reading lines, from my favorite play, with an actual actress, got me kind of giddy. I simply had to act like an actress who needed to act calm. After all, I was just pressing the speak button. *Here I go!*

This is how it went:

> LADY CAPULET
> Tell me, daughter Juliet,
> How stands your disposition to be married?

> JULIET
> It is an honor that I dream not of.

I was thinking the same thing. Marriage? At age thirteen? Gee!

> LADY CAPULET
> In brief: The valiant Paris seeks you for his love.
> What say you? Can you love the gentleman?

I was thinking, *Huh?* But I remembered this part. Parents literally "gave" their daughters in marriage—whether she loved the guy or not! Juliet basically says, "No way!" But later her mom says:

> Marry, my child,
> Early next Thursday morn,

The gallant, young and noble gentleman,
The County Paris, at Saint Peter's Church,
Shall happily make thee there a joyful bride.

Juliet then tells her mom, "No way am I gonna marry that geeky guy named Paris! I'm in love with Romeo!" or something like that.

Miss Gertie was doing an awesome job of pretending to be a mean mom who had forgotten about the joy of true love between teenagers. She was going to rock it as Lady Capulet, who had no intention of letting her teenage daughter disobey her.

So since Juliet is determined to be with her true love, Romeo, all sorts of terrible mix-ups take place. It's horrible and awesome at the same time. Her dad calls her nasty names, like "green-sickness carrion" and "tallowface"! Jeesh.

But that's why Romeo and Juliet run away and the story ends in tragedy, and I guess the parents are sorry. It's a fantastic story, the kind you never forget because it didn't have to happen that way!

CHAPTER 33

The Globe Theatre was packed! And yep, loads of people were standing. But what was WAY cool was they had a special platform just for wheelchairs! Mrs. V is going to talk about this for the rest of her life. She actually got all teary when she saw it. Because the wheelchair platform, which I could roll up, set me high enough that my head was nearly the same height as everyone else's! I could see everything! Huge major mega props to whoever thought of this. Had to be someone in a wheelchair, 'cause if you weren't, you would never come up with this idea. Truth, it made ME teary!

And the stage itself . . . was outside, in the center of

the rounded building, with the thatched roof only over the ring of audience surrounding the stage. Good thing it wasn't raining! I read in the playbill, which Mrs. V held out for me to see, that the original Globe was built by William Shakespeare's very own company, because their first theater was run by a meanie man who wouldn't renew their lease. So he and his theater buddies snuck onto the land with daggers and cudgels and swiped the timbers to remake the theater here! And they invented this rounded place so that everyone could see. Which was why it was called the Globe! So smart. Was I geeking out a little? Yeah, I was. I loved this stuff!

The music started. It sounded like an entire symphony. I couldn't see musicians anywhere, until I looked up, and there they were, up on the third tier of balconies. Flutes and violins and trumpets and even a lute!

I waited for an actor to go on stage, but instead, Mr. Hammond jogged to the center of it and bellowed out, "Welcome, welcome, ladies and gentlemen. I am particularly delighted that you have joined us for today's performance, as today—and today only—we have a very special guest.

"An actress who stepped away from the stage many years ago.

"An actress who, in her heyday, performed with the likes of Peter O'Toole, Alec Guinness, and Maggie Smith.

"An actress whose smile left no one uncharmed.

"An actress who could make us laugh, weep, gasp, and want to see that performance again and again." He opened his arms wide. "It is my honor to announce that playing the role of Lady Capulet this afternoon will be . . . Miss Gertrude Gilson."

I sure hoped Miss Gertie was hearing that applause. Now I fully understood the phrase "bring the house down." The applause was boisterous, celebratory, thundering, and resounding.

As the music rose again, I thought about how everybody knows the basics of *Romeo and Juliet*, but most don't think about it unless your teacher assigned it in class. But I loved the way English sounded back then—the fancy, old-fashioned words, and the descriptions of the sword fights and the romances and, surprisingly, lots of murders!

Romeo and Juliet had all that and a bag of chips! Two young people, not much older than me and Noah, manage to meet, fall in love, try to run away, and die tragically. I call that pretty good writing, because Shakespeare wrote it over four hundred years ago and folks are *still* reading it. And watching the play.

But *Romeo and Juliet* was more than sword fights and really old-sounding English. Mr. Shakespeare could *write*. He wrote beautiful descriptions of starlight and sunsets, and of desperation and sorrow, of the "star-crossed" lovers who tried so hard and failed to end up together. Would we still remember the play today if Juliet and Romeo had met up in time and had run away together and lived happily ever after? Doubt it.

I couldn't help but wonder if I would ever find that kind of love.

The play opened with swords being swung, then shifted to laughter as Romeo (another cutie patootie; Sky was going to break my arm with all her nudges) and his friends goofed around in the city, cracking jokes and checking out the girls, just like guys today. They battled with swords, teased each other, and acted like the boys at my school—goofy and clueless. The possibility of "true love" never entered their minds.

But then Romeo accidentally met Juliet, and because it's fiction, I guess, they fell in love, exchanged promises and sweet words, even though their parents were bitter enemies.

I was so caught up, I forgot all about Miss Gertie. So when she came onstage, I hardly recognized her. She wore a gown of emerald green covered in intricate embroidery all the way down the front. It swept to the floor. A dozen glittering necklaces hung from her neck, and what looked like a rounded velvet wreath circled her head. The wreath was a deeper green, and from the center of that popped a long veil that trailed behind her. Miss Gertie, I mean Lady Capulet, had a glint in her eyes and a defiant look on her face as she began to try to talk her daughter into marrying a guy named Paris—she did not know Juliet had already secretly married Romeo!

I could not take my eyes off Miss Gertie. It was as if she had been onstage . . . yesterday!

She tossed her head and spoke out firmly, just as she'd practiced: "Tell me, daughter Juliet / How stands your disposition to be married?"

Juliet replied politely, "It is an honor that I dream not of."

(In other words: "The thought has not crossed my mind! Are you crazy, Mom? I'm THIRTEEN!")

But her mom proceeded to tell her she was being married off anyway, to some guy she didn't know and for sure didn't love!

The play continued. The squabbling parents. The sweet words between Juliet and Romeo, him calling to her as she stood above on her balcony. The kiss! (I looked at Sky, she looked at me, and I could tell she was thinking of that kid Billy Shakespeare, just like I was thinking of Noah.)

The rest of the play was, well, you have to see it! Sword fights! Tears! Tragedy! Romeo and Juliet both die at the end. I knew that of course, but still it hit me hard. These were kids who got caught up in a situation that got out of their control. I saw tears on Sky's cheeks. And on Mrs. V's. And felt them on my own.

When the last act finished, the applause was loud, tremendous, bellowing!

Miss Gertie got called back for FIVE curtain calls! I felt ridiculously happy for her. She bowed gracefully, wept real tears, and thanked everyone profusely.

"And now I know why this theater is so packed," Sky gushed.

"It's all too beautiful for words!" I tapped, aware of the irony I'd just typed. I thought we'd find Miss Gertie, then leave with the crowds, but Oliver caught up to tell us that Mr. Hammond wanted to give us a quick tour of the place. We met Miss Gertie backstage; her face was beaming, her eyes shining. I have never seen such joy. There were many hugs and compliments and giggles of satisfaction, with Mr. Hammond coming over to join in, before he began our tour.

The costume room especially made me flat-out dizzy. I wheeled past Henry VIII's royal robes, Lady Macbeth's gowns, the flowers Ophelia wore in her hair, Oberon's and Titania's fairy costumes, Othello's swords. Sky looked at me and wiggled her eyebrows, as if daring me to start another duel, and we broke out in giggles. Soooo many costumes! And . . . we got to try some on! Sky turned me into Puck, a fairy from *A Midsummer Night's Dream*, and she put on the donkey ears of Nick Bottom, a character who'd had his head transformed into a donkey's by Puck. Mrs. V struck a pose with a sword held high, and Oliver snapped away. Then he pulled Sky over to the Antony and Cleopatra costumes. He slipped on Antony's toga and had Sky swap out the donkey ears for Cleopatra's gown, and Mrs. V took a photo of them while they had a huge make-believe screaming match, to send to their parents!

When we finally left the Globe, Mr. Hammond insisted that Miss Gertie was welcome back onstage at any time— just give him a ring. I suddenly remembered that Teddy was waiting for us, but now we were an hour late. I felt an instant pang. I didn't know how we would ever find him again. But as we made our way to the exit, there was a black cab, a man waving gallantly from the window. Teddy!

We thanked him for waiting, thanked Oliver again for getting us the tickets, then piled in, gushing about the play. And of course, about Miss Gertie's unexpected performance. Teddy slapped his hand against his forehead.

"And I missed it? Oh, what I'd give to see you onstage again," he said, his voice sincere as could be.

I looked to Miss Gertie, who was still sort of glowing, and I suspected Teddy's words had something to do with it.

"Well, if you give me your card, I shall ring you up if I take up the director's kind invitation to return," she told him.

"Happy to!" Then he turned for a quick look at her at the stoplight. "You're here for a few more days—perhaps I could treat you and Mrs. V to some fish-and-chips, when these young folk are out and about? There's a beauty of a place not far from here by the name of Finley's— freshest haddock this side of Grimsby."

Sky and I gaped at each other. This was FATE. Finley's was Miss Gertie's favorite place! Miss Gertie looked surprised as well, in a good way.

Mrs. V looked . . . mischievous. "Gertie and I would love to," she answered quickly, before Miss Gertie could say a word.

CHAPTER 34

Crossing over the river Thames on our way back to the hotel, Teddy took a slight detour to drive us by the Tower of London. That was where the Crown Jewels were—and people got to see them! Teddy said they were worth billions of dollars.

"What if someone stole them?" I typed.

"You'd be caught in an instant," Teddy scoffed. "First off, they're tucked away behind bulletproof glass. Second, there are over a hundred cameras watching that part of the tower. And third, there's a small army of guards. Mind you, there was one attempt. That was back in the 1700s! One of the safest places to be in London—the tower."

That was interesting, as I knew that the tower had also been used as a prison, and once held two little princes, one who should have become king, who disappeared and were probably murdered—they say by their uncle, who wanted to be the king instead. *They* sure hadn't been safe!

"Can we go tomorrow?" I asked Mrs. V, Sky wholeheartedly nodding in agreement.

"Let's first see what else is on our list—most of the tower is hundreds of years old, with winding, narrow steps and levels. When they built it, they weren't thinking about tourism or wheelchair accessibility," Mrs. V told us almost apologetically.

Well, I couldn't get annoyed about that. There was so much else to do anyway, and from our drive by, I did spy some of the ravens on the tower walls, and yep, they really were humongous. Teddy said they had their wings clipped a bit so they wouldn't fly away—the saying was that if there are ever less than six ravens in the tower, the kingdom will fall! But they probably wouldn't fly off regardless, as they were so well-fed. Huh. They couldn't get out, and I couldn't get in. Something to think about.

It was nearing six by the time Teddy dropped us off at the Marlington. Miss Gertie wasn't the only one a "bit knackered," as she called it. Even my thumb was tired;

Sky had to push me into the elevator. Jet lag is no joke!

Channel 12 had told us all our meals were covered, including room service, so we ordered from the menu in our room. Yikes, it was expensive! Mrs. V said it was thoughtful of me to worry about the bill, but I need to eat more for dinner than mushy peas! This time I chose shepherd's pie, which was sort of like hamburger and mashed potatoes cooked in a pie crust. It was delicious and a perfectly soft companion to my mushy peas. Sky and Mrs. V ordered something called Cornish pasties, which had beef and little cubes of turnip and potato and parsnip (which I learned was like a really sweet white carrot) and onion, wrapped into a crust shaped sort of like an empanada. Miss Gertie ordered roast beef, which she ate half of and declared the day had "tuckered" her out, she couldn't chew another bite. But we all had room for dessert!

We were in the middle of making plans for the next day when Sky's phone sang out. I did a little shimmy to the Double Trouble tune as Sky answered.

"Hey, Oliver. . . . Yep, we just ate. . . . Am I still sitting down? Yeah, why?"

Now I was getting really nosy! Especially when a millisecond later Sky was no longer sitting down, but shooting her fist, then herself, into the air.

"What, what??!!" I wanted to know.

"Really? REALLY, REALLY?" Sky was looking at me wildly, mouth as wide open as mine sometimes is.

What, what, what!!

"Mom and Dad got them? Really?" And finally, she mouthed, "Double Trouble tickets, for tomorrow" to me.

If I weren't belted into my chair, I would have shot right into the air, too. What universe was this? No way, no way, I'd heard wrong. There was no way! But Sky was saying, "Okay, let me see if they're cool with it, and I'll call you back. Oliver, you are the best! Well, so are Mom and Dad!"

Sky tapped her phone off and spun around, then grasped Miss Gertie's hand. "My parents! They somehow got tickets for me and Oliver and Melody as a surprise! To see Double Trouble! Can we go? Please, can we?"

I shrieked. I shriek quite a bit—it's simply one of the noises that erupts from my mouth without any effort on my part. But this was an honest-to-goodness real gut-scream of joy! *Double Trouble?!* Like I said, they were the hottest, cutest band in the universe! Marco was originally from Trinidad, while Ian was born in Scotland and was half Ethiopian. They were a couple of years older than Sky, always wore ripped black jeans and high-tops and sometimes blazers, and super-skinny ties that they'd throw into the audience. And their voices, ahhhh—they shifted from sweet and easy to growly, and they. Were.

So. Good. Kids would literally camp out overnight to get tickets to their concerts. I had three of their albums downloaded on Elvira. Sky told me she had all seven.

The DT boys, as they were sometimes called, were *always* hitting the number one spot on ZibberZabber. They sang pop rock and a little bit of rap, and I hummed them in my head all the time, like a silent soundtrack.

Mrs. V and Miss Gertie glanced at each other. They saw my legs kicking and kicking. "Well, I can tell this is a big deal," Miss Gertie said, "but what exactly is Double Trouble?"

"Band band favorite band!" I typed.

Sky started dancing with my hands. "Number one favorite! And it's totally impossible to get tickets! But my parents found out they're playing in London for the next few days, and my dad knows someone who knows someone or something and somehow got us tickets! Please, can we go? Oliver will be with us!"

Mrs. V had that mischievous look on her face again. "Oh, so your great-aunt and I aren't invited?"

Sky stopped short. "Oh! Um, well—"

Mrs. V took pity on her by quickly saying it wasn't her "thing."

"Please pleeeeeeaase can we go?" I tapped. Me watching Double Trouble LIVE? I was having trouble thinking!

"Well, I'd need to check in with your parents first, Melody, but since you'll be with Oliver. . . . What time would it be, Sky?"

"At six tomorrow. They're doing two back-to-back sets in a smaller hall. Then they play at the big stadium, Wembley, over the weekend."

A phone call home later (which was filled with more *Miss You*s and *Are You Having Fun*s than actual conversation about Double Trouble), and yes, YES, Sky and I were going to a DOUBLE TROUBLE concert. I guess I fell asleep that night, but I was so excited I couldn't stop kicking. I felt bad for Sky, but she said it was no big deal—her *heart* was kicking. HA.

The moment I woke up on Friday, I was thinking DOUBLE TROUBLE. Were we really going to see them, live? For real? I didn't think I could focus on a single other thing all day. But when Mrs. V trundled us out of the hotel that morning after "a proper English breakfast," which was fried tomatoes and mushrooms along with eggs and sausage, and of course tea, I discovered I was still distractable. At least by a library.

Libraries are my happy place. Well, Target, too, but libraries even more. I'm a reader kid. I love books! If you can't talk and you can't walk, but you love stories, you learn to hang out at the library—a lot. My parents or

Mrs. V take Penny and me almost every week. Yep, we're regulars at our local branch. And that was how I found out about my summer camp, which, hello, was the best thing I'd ever done in my life, until, maybe now. I mean, DOUBLE TROUBLE. Hello. Just joking! But, yeah, def my happy place.

And if you're wondering why we'd go to a library here when we go all the time anyway? This library, the London Library, was a whole other league. I think about a hundred of my libraries could fit into it. It didn't look massive from the outside—very neat and orderly, with elegant white columns. But once you were inside . . . it went on and on and on. Shelves and stacks filled with secrets and knowledge. I felt myself buzzing. I could live here, camp out in the back, and gulp the knowledge from all those shelves.

"It's like a house of mirrors," Sky breathed, looking out at all the books.

Miss Gertie sighed happily. "My gran took me here all the time, just after it was rebuilt."

"Rebuilt?" I typed.

"During World War II," Miss Gertie said, her face going serious, "a good part of London was bombed. The library was devasted by a shell. If memory serves, over sixteen thousand books were destroyed."

I thought that over, how many books that was. What

if some were the only ones in existence? Those words would be gone forever! We all went quiet for a moment, feeling that loss, I could tell. But then we were itching to start exploring.

Some of the wooden bookcases looked ancient—they must have survived the bombing. They stood regally beside sleek computer worktables. Curved metal staircases led to even more books on shelves that literally reached the ceiling. "A million books, and nineteen miles of shelves," a librarian murmured to us. Whaaaa? I didn't even know how to think about that.

Miss Gertie laughed when the librarian told us those numbers. "That's a bit too much walking for me."

I gotta admit I'd been worried about how Miss Gertie would do after her fall, but I shouldn't have been. As long as we didn't walk too far, and had short rests in between, she was good to go. Had I thought she wouldn't do well because of the fall, though, or because of her age? Maybe a little of both? I watched as she trailed her hand along a row of poetry collections. Her face was as eager-looking as a child's. Jeesh, it made me so mad when people made assumptions about me because of the way I looked. And here I was doing the same with Miss Gertie! Hopefully, she had no idea I was thinking that, because I wasn't going to any longer. And I hadn't thought that way until she'd fallen. But anyone could fall. The idea that you could fall and no one would know—that was the scariest part. I was beyond grateful that I'd seen Miss Gertie from my window!

The same librarian strode silently over to me. "Let me know if you'd like to see anything from the upper stacks," he said. "It's my joy to connect a book with its reader." I appreciated that. Those stacks were high!

I had Sky buy Mrs. V a London Library tote bag for me—I would give it to her as a thank-you gift when we got home. We basically did not want to leave this place. Ever! But London was calling; there was lots more to see.

CHAPTER 35

Like Trafalgar Square. The column in the center was so tall I couldn't crane my head back far enough to see who was perched on top of it, but boy, that statue had a pretty great view. Even better were the four massive stone lions guarding him. I looked at the plaque. Lord Nelson. Who, hmm, I didn't know a lot about, actually. But I thought England didn't belong to France because of something he did. So I guess he deserved the tallest statue. No wonder those lions were protecting it! Lots of kids and teenagers were climbing up the pedestal and sitting on the lions, parents and friends snapping away.

"**You go up, Sky! Mrs. V can take your picture,**" I told my friend.

Sky looked stricken. "But you can't go up!"

"**It's okay. I can**"—I looked around—"**create a pigeon cloud!**" Then I pushed my speed to its fastest and rode through the square, scattering hundreds of pigeons, just like the little kids were doing. They watched me, laughing and clapping. I spun back around and grinned.

"Okay, fine!" So she hopped onto that pedestal, and lay across one of the lions' backs, pretending to be asleep. I loved that Sky didn't do what the other kids were doing—roaring at the lions. But sometimes, I really liked being able to do what the other kids were doing. I'm good at squealing, so I opened my mouth wide and gave a roar! And you know what? That felt *good*!

And that's when I heard it, a sound that was even more eerie and otherworldly and perfectly delicious than when I'd looked it up before the trip. A bagpipe! I felt almost haunted, in the best way; haunted by music that sounded from beyond time. A man was playing at the other end of the square. I wheeled over and listened until at last the others came over.

"Ah, it's a lovely sound, isn't it?" Miss Gertie said. Then she added, with one of her mysterious looks on her face, "Are any of you ladies feeing a bit peckish?"

"A bit what?" Sky asked.

Miss Gertie laughed. "Hungry. I know I am! Shall we nip into a pastry shop and have some high tea?"

"There are levels of tea?" I typed.

Miss Gertie drew herself up like the actress that she was. "All will be revealed."

What was revealed was . . . a sweet tooth's nirvana. Penny's head was going to explode when I told her about THIS. We sat in this dining room that was straight-out-of-a-magazine pretty. White tablecloths and billowy white flowers that smelled like jasmine and something nirvana-ish. The waiters were dressed in white. The plates and teacups were white with tiny blue polka dots on the edges. Mrs. V made sure we were seated at a corner table so that people wouldn't see me being fed, which I mega appreciated. Not that anyone was paying one iota of attention to me, because . . .

Ohhhhh my gosh. Out came gleaming silver teapots, one for each of us! And then, and THEN, our waiter brought out two triple-tiered cake stands and set them onto our table with a "Ta-da!" One stand held three levels of tiny layered sandwiches—practically doll-sized. Some were made with white bread and some were a darker brown bread, and each layer had a different filling. Cucumbers? Something orange? And on the top, in the center, was a single white bowl, surrounded by those puffy white flowers, with a mashed-up sandwich, just for me. But that wasn't even the most exciting part.

The second arched stand held tiers of the teeniest, tiniest, fanciest cakes and desserts I'd ever seen. Sky had her phone out, taking close-ups, as soon as that stand landed on our table. And now I got why everything else was white—those desserts were the stars of the show. Tiny strips of graham cracker crust with mango soufflé sitting on top, with a curl of meringue on top of that. Even tinier shortbread cookies shaped like ice-cream cones, a dot of frosting indicating the "flavors." Pyramids of grasshopper-green minty cheesecake, chocolate shavings on top. Pop-in-your-mouth-sized scones. And a dessert that was, no joke, shaped like a fancy high-heeled shoe, polka-dotted to match the plates. And the shoe stood up! Yep, nirvana. And most of the desserts were soft, or could be soaked for a second in milk, so I could try them all. I even tried the one with the chocolate shavings. Sky informed me that I was very brave. I agreed.

There were so many choices we couldn't eat them all!

"Can we bring the rest back to the hotel?" Sky asked. I could hardly nod fast enough.

"I think Melody isn't the only one who'll be rolling out of here," Mrs. V joked as she patted her belly a half hour later.

"I don't think I can eat anything else for the rest of the trip!" Miss Gertie agreed.

"Sooooo . . . ," Sky started, in a way that let me know she was up to something. "How about we walk our food off, do a little window-shopping? And *maybe* we might see something that'd be fun to wear to the concert tonight?"

With our leftover goodies tucked into a white-ribboned (of course) box, off we went, popping into shops on King's Road, which had more stores than I'd ever seen in my life.

CHAPTER 36

"What look are we going for?" I asked Sky as we left the fourth store in a row without buying anything. The clothes were ah-mazing, but they were nutty expensive. Mrs. V looked stunned by the prices!

"Hmm. How about a little retro? A little vintage? Ohhh, look, a thrift shop!"

"Let's try that." I'd heard of thrift shops—you could find the coolest used clothes there. I was already thinking I'd wear my black leggings that night. Then Sky spied some low boots called Doc Martens, way cooler than any shoes I had. She knelt down and in a very posh British voice said, "Allow me, m'lady!" And my legs stayed still, and whaddaya know, the boots fit perfectly. I already felt cooler! Sky then snatched up about twenty items, slipped behind a curtain, and gave Miss Gertie, Mrs. V, and me a quick fashion show.

"I want honesty!" she demanded as she waltzed back out.

"That's a B-plus," I said about a tank top that had some cute anime characters on the front.

"You look like a . . . potato in that!" This was about a tan sack-like dress that might've looked awesome on someone about six feet tall, wearing six-inch heels.

"Why did I even tell you to be honest?" Sky teased. "But seriously, be honest!" We cracked up. She finally came out wearing super-wide-legged pants, a super-wide belt, and a sea-green sleeveless top that looked awesome with her red hair streaks.

"THAT rocks!"

"Cool. And all together it's only about thirty pounds, which is . . ."

"Forty-two dollars." Yeah, figuring out exchange rates is the same as most math—I can do it in my head. Sky and I pawed through a few more racks of clothes until we found a sort of baby-doll top made of soft, rose-colored linen, with thin straps, which Sky insisted was great with my hair. Mrs. V helped me get it over my T-shirt, and even like that, I knew it was perfect.

Sky hopped from foot to foot excitedly. "Just need a choker type of necklace, and you are set, girl!" She found a bin of jewelry and pulled out a leather choker with chunky beads on it. "Three pounds!" And we were DONE.

Mrs. V insisted we go back to the hotel and rest up before Oliver brought us to the concert. Let's just say it's hard to rest when you are SUPREMELY EXCITED.

"I still can't believe it!" I typed to Sky.

Sky agreed. "Kids actually fly from other countries to see DT!"

"Ha, so did we!"

"I wonder how close our seats are," she mused. Then she decided, "Doesn't matter. Breathing the same air as them is enough." Mrs. V and Miss Gertie looked at each other and held back their laughs.

Finally, finally, finalllllllllly, we ate an early dinner— I just had oatmeal because my belly was big-time fluttering—then put on our new-old thrift clothes.

"These boots rock," I typed to Sky, looking down at my feet. And the top fit perfectly—it floated gently as I moved, and Sky was right, the color was great. The choker was the finishing touch. I felt like a total teenager! Sky took forever getting ready because she kept rearranging the red spike streaks. She'd peer in close to the mirror, pull and tuck and scrunch and mush, then step away, frown, and do it all over again.

"I feel sorry for your hair!" I tapped to her.

"You got jokes!" was her answer.

Oliver showed up, and she still wasn't done. "Yeah, that's Sky," he said with a shrug. "That's why I showed up early! Else we'd be late."

When she finally came out of the bathroom, she struck a pose, chin up, head tilted, one leg forward, hands propped on hips. Yeah, she looked like she was going to a Double Trouble concert.

And after ten million Be Carefuls and Have Funs and Come Right Back Afterward Because You Have Day One of the Conference Tomorrows from Mrs. V and Miss Gertie, we actually *were* going to a Double Trouble concert.

CHAPTER 37

The line to get in was five people wide and two blocks long. Which meant that we got into the line only a block from our hotel—turned out this venue was only three blocks away. Everyone looked as excited as we were. A lot of the kids seemed about our age or a little older, but there were some younger kids—mostly girls—in line with a parent, as well as kids more Oliver's age, and even some groups of grown-ups.

"I saw them in Paris back in December," a girl wearing hoop earrings half the size of her head was telling a boy in a Duran Duran T-shirt.

"That T-shirt's vintage," Sky whispered to me.

"Huh?" I tapped.

"That's an eighties band, so the T-shirt is from that time period. Very cool!" Oliver low-voiced. Ahhh, I wondered if that kid got it at the same thrift shop we were at this afternoon!

The crowd got thicker and people got more hyper as we got closer. A group of guys were playing air guitar as a girl with a really pretty, growly voice sang "Get You Back," one of DT's bigger hits. Sooo many kids had on Double Trouble T-shirts!

Some kids in front of us must have heard Elvira's American accent, because they asked where we were from. One said she'd gone to DT concerts in New York and in Shanghai. Talk about a fangirl!

"Cool board," one guy said about Elvira. "My friend's little brother has something like that, but simpler, cuz he's only seven." That made me feel good for that kid— Elvira quite literally changed my life!

I'd never been anywhere so crowded! But as I got used to all the people, I was hoping I wouldn't bash into anyone's knees. At the same time, the crowds made everything even more exciting. All these kids, all jazzed up about the exact same thing, and me right there with them.

"You good, Melody?" Oliver asked. He kept weaving

in between me and other people if we got too close. He must have been worried about knee bashing too. I nodded. I was great.

It seemed to take forever, but the front of the line was finally in sight. Two super-burly identically dressed men were shouting, "Have your tickets out!"

I glanced up at Oliver. He winked and pulled them out of the wallet in his back pocket. I looked up at Sky; she was big-time cheesing. I could hear sound checks going on inside. There were only ten people in front of us. Then three.

Then . . .

We were at the entrance! One ticket collector was in a bright orange dress and had orange feathers in her hair. The other wore super-tight black-and-white checkered jeans and a silvery silky shirt opened up to his belly button. I was so busy looking at them, it didn't register that they had paused.

Then it did. They looked at me, strange expressions on their faces. My heart started to thud.

"Get the manager," one whispered to the other. We were asked to step to the side, then the orange feather lady dashed off. My heart thudded harder.

"Is there a problem, sir?" Oliver asked, politeness masking what I knew was concern.

"Just a moment—" No . . . no, no, no . . .

A woman wearing a Bluetooth headset strode up, speaking quickly into the mic. "Got it. Just so you know, I hate this part of my job, Nigel—"

Now she looked at me, Oliver, Sky. *No, no, no, no, no.* Her face was so full of sympathy that I could already guess what she was going to say. And then she said it.

"I can't begin to tell you how sorry I am, but"—she took a deep breath—"but . . . this hall is from the 1900s and isn't wheelchair accessible yet. We actually just got approval from the city, and funds from a very generous donor, to create an elevator, but it won't be ready for another year."

Sky grasped my hand. Oliver stepped forward. "Do you mean my friend can't go in?" No, no, no, no, no . . .

"I'm so sorry! But it's against safety regulations. We'd never want to put even one of our concertgoers into a position of danger."

"But . . . but . . . couldn't a bunch of us carry her in?" Oliver asked, desperation seeping into his voice. A few guys near us, clearly listening, instantly chimed in, offering to help.

The woman looked from them to me, then squatted down beside me. "Sweetheart, we can't risk anything happening to you going up those stairs, or even inside. There isn't enough room for a wheelchair like yours to maneuver around comfortably, or get out quickly if for some terrible reason a fire broke out. Again, I'm so sorry."

Sky stood frozen. My insides were curdling.

"There's really nothing we can do?" Oliver pleaded.

The woman thought for a moment. "Unfortunately, the website clearly stated that this venue was not wheelchair accessible—I feel terribly that you missed that. But I can make sure you are fully reimbursed. And I can get you all free T-shirts!"

No, no, no, no, no, no, no, no, no.

No, no, no, no, no, no, no, no, no.

I had to leave. I had to leave right now. With my chest so tight I thought it would split open, arms shaking, I managed somehow to type:

"Sky. Oliver. Go see show. I will leave. I need to leave. NOW." I tugged at Sky's arm. I reached for Oliver. Sky's eyes were filling with tears; she was furiously blinking them back. "We all go or none of us go," she said, jaw set firm.

Oliver said to the woman, "I'll be back about the tickets. . . . We need to leave. I realize this isn't your fault, but it really sucks."

"It really does," she said, pushing her hair from her brow, which had broken out into a sweat. "Wait—maybe, maybe we can exchange your tickets for a later date? When the boys' tour returns? I believe they're back in October. . . ."

Leave leave leave! I flicked at the toggle on my chair, but by now my arm was shaking so hard with my fury and sadness that I couldn't hit it. I tried again and again.

"That's kind of you, but they're visiting from the States. . . ." Oliver laid a hand on each of my wheelchair bars. "I got you, Melody," he said.

Sky took my shaking hand. "Me too."

The walk back to the hotel was the worst. The weight of feeling guilty, MAD, embarrassed, and even jealous of everyone else who was getting to be at the concert felt like drowning. Drowning inside myself. I knew it wasn't the concert people's fault. Oliver kept trying to cheer me up, cheer Sky up, saying he'd figure out something else awesome to do while we were here. Sky kept telling me it wasn't my fault, but her voice was so quavery that I felt even more guilty because she was being so nice!

My brain was churning every detail over—doing its best not to let the rest of me start crying. It spent a lot of time on *the hall isn't wheelchair accessible.* Brain snapshots brought me back to inching forward in the crowd, the kids singing and air guitaring, the kids in their Double Trouble T-shirts. And, huh, none of those snapshots showed anyone else in a wheelchair. All those people in that massive line, and I was the only one. But it wasn't

Sky's parents' fault! People don't look for that type of information unless it affects them in some way.

Oliver must have been in my mind yet again, because he said, "I'm really sorry that my folks didn't know about the problem with the hall—"

I flung out an arm to stop him. **"It's not their fault,"** I finally typed, tears I was blinking back burning my eyes.

CHAPTER 38

I made it all the way to the hotel lobby before I started to cry. We were back exactly where we'd started, while everyone else we'd been in line with was now waiting for the band to come onstage. I wasn't crying just because I'd wanted to see Double Trouble so badly. Though I wanted to soooo badly. And I wasn't crying because it made me think of that time I was left behind by my class-mates on the trip for the Whiz Kids championship—this time, I wasn't alone. I had Sky, and Oliver. But because of ME, Sky didn't get to see the concert either. If I hadn't been there, they'd both be at the concert! It *was* my fault!

It was taking all my willpower not to start full-on

sobbing. If I did, I'd make noises that I couldn't stop, and the lobby was full of people, so I fought the tears back. I couldn't take even more people staring at me. But I couldn't stop the tears; I couldn't even wipe them away.

We hurried through, Oliver jabbing at the button for the elevator, telling us he was going to run back and get reimbursed for our tickets after we got settled upstairs. "We will do something crazy fun with that money," he swore again. When the elevator opened, he helped Sky wheel me in. Just as it was closing, we heard someone shout, "Hold the door!"

Sky slapped at the open button. The guy stuck his arm between the doors. The doors opened up again. The guy jumped in.

"Ta, mate!" he said, bending toward the buttons, hitting the one for the penthouse. Then he turned to us . . .

. . . he turned to us . . . and we saw a flop of dark-brown hair, a chiseled jaw, high cheekbones, a tiny scar under his left eye, glinting brown eyes . . . two silver studs in one ear . . .

And I think I went into shock. My whole body locked up; not even one leg kicked.

Ian Murphy of Double Trouble was in the elevator with us! And he was saying, "Really appreciate it, mate. Left my phone in the room; Marco's ready to shoot me—we're already bloody late!"

Tears were still running down my face. All I could think was Ian Murphy from Double Trouble was in the elevator with us, and here I was crying!

"No problem," Sky managed to croak out as the door shut and the elevator started to move. She was trying not to stare. I couldn't not stare. I think my neck forgot how to work.

"Always forgetting my phone—" he went on, brushing back his hair and grinning. Then he paused. Looked at my face. Looked to Oliver and Sky.

"Are . . . you okay? Do you need any . . . help?" he asked. I snuffled hard, begging my legs not to kick.

"We, uh, we, um, well, we . . . ," Sky started.

Oliver finished for her. "We were headed to your, uh, concert, in fact, and, my parents had gotten us tickets, and they didn't realize that Square Hall can't accommodate these types of wheelchairs. So, we, uh—" Oliver almost finished.

Ian waited. Oliver and Sky looked at each other— I could tell they were worried about what to say that wouldn't get me upset all over again. *And how slow is this elevator?* I thought.

"They wouldn't let me in," I typed.

"WHAT?!" said Ian, aghast. "That's bloody ridiculous. That's—that's—there should be a law!" He smacked his head. "Never even considered that, gotta admit. Okay, let me think." He drummed his fingers against the elevator door, then spun around.

"First, cheers. I'm Ian, and it's very nice to meet you."

Sky, despite looking thunderstruck, managed to say, "I'm Sky, and this is my brother, Oliver—" Then she waved her hand toward me.

But before she could say my name, I tapped out, **"I'm Melody. A total fangirl."**

Ian threw his head back and laughed. "Okay, fangirl. First, I want to apologize on behalf of Double Trouble and the venue. We would have loved having you at our show. Tell you what—ride up with me, let me get my phone, and then I'm calling my manager. . . . I have an idea." He laughed again. "Man, Marco is going to KILL me; we're gonna be sooo late."

"No way anyone leaves. They will wait all night for you," I tapped. Ian flashed me his signature double-dimpled grin, and if I'd been standing, I would have fallen flat. As the elevator finally dinged for the penthouse, Sky and I looked at each other in utter disbelief. We just met Ian Murphy from Double Trouble!

We held the elevator for a second time as Ian dashed out and into the penthouse—the elevator doors opened right into his private hallway! A piano stood at the far end of the one room I could see into. Meanwhile, Sky helped me quickly wipe the tears away. Even though we were both in shock, she was still nice enough to know that I probably wouldn't want to talk to Ian of Double Trouble with snot on my face!

Moments later, Ian jogged back, phone in one hand, a maroon baseball cap in the other. He was already talking to someone, his manager, I guessed. I tried to piece together what he was saying—something about the venue, and outraged, and fans should never be turned away, and more outraged, and what about the recording session, was that accessible? And a yes! And what day was that again?

He jammed his phone into his pocket. Folded his arms. And asked what we were doing on Monday. And had we ever been to recording session before?

CHAPTER 39

Mrs. V and Miss Gertie were instantly alarmed when they opened the door to our room and saw Sky, Oliver, and me—we'd left only an hour ago. Mrs. V scanned my face—I knew she noticed my eyes, puffy and red. But that further confused her, I could tell, because Sky and I were talking over each other in excitement.

"We couldn't get in!"

"We met them. Well, one of them!"

"The place couldn't allow wheelchairs!"

"Ian was SO nice!"

"We can't see the concert, that's why we're back!"

"We were so mad!"

"But the Double Trouble guys invited us to a . . ."

"RECORDING SESSION," I typed as Sky and Oliver mind-melded with me, shouting it at the same time.

"They said someone with a name like Melody would bring them good luck!" Sky said with a blast of sass. I grinned just thinking about it.

Miss Gertie and Mrs. V stared at us as if we'd lost our minds, Miss Gertie quipping, "That was in English, but I don't understand a single word of it!"

Oliver quickly ran through the entire story, and now I got to see the same reactions we'd experienced since we'd first gotten into line, but on other people's faces. They were excited, worried, upset, angry, teary, surprised, then excited again. Well, ha-ha, excited for *us* when they heard that the band, wanting to make it right, had invited us to join them at their recording studio on Monday to watch them work on a new song. And the studio was modern, wheelchairs welcomed.

We hadn't lost our minds. We were out-of-our-minds psyched. It sucked scissors that we couldn't go to the concert, but getting to watch Double Trouble, be right near them, maybe even talk to them again, was going to be even better!

"Plus! Melody! We're going to hear a song no other kid in the WORLD has ever heard before! This is MEGA!" Sky blurted out. And you know what, she was right. Double Trouble could come to the States one day, and play somewhere near us—there'd always be another chance to see their concert. But this? It was like taking a dream and having it turn into the stratosphere!

After freaking out about Double Trouble some more, listening to our favorite songs, and convincing Mrs. V and Miss Gertie to let us go on Monday, Mrs. V reminded me that I should probably think about heading to bed. The I.D.E.A. symposium was first thing in the morning—a fact that had been temporarily driven from my mind because of DOUBLE TROUBLE!

I dutifully began looking up more information about I.D.E.A. Keeping so busy the past few days had helped me forget my biggest fear: Why had they chosen me? What could I possibly be contributing to this that all these older kids with their accomplishments couldn't? And now that it was tomorrow, the WHY ME went high volume. Miss Gertie and Sky asked if I wanted to watch some funny oldie British TV show with them, one that Sky kept having laughing spasms over it.

But I couldn't concentrate on TV. I was too busy panicking because suddenly my brain was full of WHY MEs. I finally turned to ask Mrs. V, who was doing yoga on the carpet.

"Because you are smarter, braver, more thoughtful, and more full of ideas and curiosity than most people who have a far easier time navigating the world than you do." She folded her arms and pursed her lips, appraising me. "And most people can't possibly fully understand what will make life easier for people who are more challenged, because they don't live it day to day. It's like—"

"It's like how a giraffe knows the tops of trees, but not under a bush." I gave my hand a shake, kept typing. **"And how a fox knows what's under a bush, but not the tops of trees?"**

"Exactly. Excellent metaphor, by the way." Mrs. V gazed at me fondly. "They don't just want you, they *need* you. Remember: they didn't have to invite you. You'd never even have known about it. They made a choice, and they chose you, based on everything that you are. So every time the 'Why Me' pops up, chant 'They Chose Me.' Okay?"

I took a beat to think about that. They chose me. They chose *me.*

"Okay."

CHAPTER 40

It was early. The time when I liked to think before the day begins. Last night was so totally terrible and so supremely wonderful! But as I lay there in bed, I wasn't even sure I was supposed to be here in London, England, at all. I was a girl from Ohio in the USA, a girl who couldn't walk or talk or do diddly by herself. Yet somehow, I was a zillion miles away from home, in a country I wasn't familiar with—a country with cool sights and lots of juicy history—and I was supposed to be participating in this symposium on top of *that*. I wasn't even a teenager yet! And everyone else would be!

Yeah, I was kinda freaking out. And probably I

shouldn't have spent so much time deep-diving on the internet about I.D.E.A.!

Probably to torture myself, I started to think about famous people I admired who overcame impossible odds. Stevie Wonder was blind, and he became a famous singer. Helen Keller changed the world for folks like me. Stephen Hawking was a genius in a wheelchair with less control over his body than me, and he figured out atomic math calculations that most brains, including mine, can't fathom.

Jeez. Sure, I struggle through stuff, but I'm nothing like them.

I huffed out a breath—a combination sigh and muffled screech, all my fear and frustration exploding from my gut. The WHY MEs were flexing big-time, scaring off the THEY CHOSE YOUs.

"Feeling nervous?" Sky asked softly. Shoot, did I wake her up?

I nodded.

"Good! That means you're for real." She raised herself up on one elbow. "How could you not be intimidated? If I couldn't talk, and then somebody told me that I had to be in this conference, and somehow create some brilliant idea, I'd make like lightning and *bolt*, girl."

I smiled at her understanding.

"Seriously, I'd probably wet my pants!"

Now I laughed.

"But I get it, I do." I studied her; her voice was soft, her eyebrows slightly furrowed. "There's actually an expression for that," Sky continued. "Impostor syndrome!"

"What's that?" I typed.

"When you feel like you don't deserve to be where you belong!"

"You feel like that too?"

"Sometimes." She pulled the sheet up over her nose. "I kind of sometimes feel like that because I'm never anywhere for very long; I don't actually belong *anywhere*."

"But can't you tell your parents?" I typed, feeling so badly for her.

Sky pulled the sheet higher.

"Sky???"

She lowered the sheet an inch. "It's just . . . they're helping so many people. How can I complain about *that*?" Now her voice had a quaver to it.

"It's not complaining. You matter most to them! Maybe they have no clue; they think you're fine." I nodded hard at her, went to pat her hand but whacked her elbow. **"Oops! Sorry!"**

"No worries," Sky said. "And maybe you're right. Maybe I should tell them. How can they know if I don't, right?"

"Brave up, girlfriend," I typed.

"Then *you* brave up, girlfriend! You were picked to go to this thing for a reason, Melody. Yeah, it'll be intense, but seems to me that they think you can handle it."

Just what Mrs. V said. Okay. Fine. They chose me. They chose me. They chose ME.

But why ME? Brain, stopppppppppppp!

Mrs. V had showered me and washed my hair last night, so getting ready in the morning was easy-peasy. Good thing, because Sky decided she wanted to change her spike color, then hop in the shower, and wow, can that girl shower.

"Did you leave any water for the rest of the hotel?" I teased.

"Hey, early birds get the . . . longest showers?"

"Sad, sad, sad."

Sky stuck her tongue out at me. Then she began towel-drying her hair so hard I wondered if there'd be any hair left when she was through. I hoped so—I wanted to see what color she used today! Mrs. V put on my white jeans and new white sneakers again, a pale blue T-shirt that had pretty dark-blue birds and flowers embroidered all around the neck, and dangly earrings. I looked at myself in the mirror. Yes! I looked like a teenager again! And the birds, they kinda looked like Mrs. V's blue jays.

I hoped they were doing okay on their own without Mrs. V there spoiling them.

Miss Gertie was on the phone with another great-niece, who lived a town over; she and her husband were going to pick her and Sky up and bring them to visit Bath, an ancient town with actual Roman baths literally from the Roman times, for the day.

"Yes, the Marlington Hotel. I can't wait to see all of you! It's been too many years! Little Benny is at university?" She clucked her tongue. "Excuse me . . . Benjamin! He was in diapers when I last saw him.

"Oh my. It really has been such a long time. But it feels marvelous to be back in London again. See you soon!"

As she clicked off her phone, she relaxed back in her chair with a smile. This made me smile; she looked so . . . content. She leaned toward me. "Family is everything, Melody. Never forget that. I've been away for too long. Far too long. I truly don't know how I stayed away . . . from everyone—no, the world—for all these years." She gazed out the window at another bright day in London—I think all those guidebooks saying it always rained needed updating! "I . . . I wasn't sure who I was anymore after I lost Jasper. I decided to stop acting. And the longer I kept to myself, the harder it became to go back out into the world."

"It's easy to want to hide," I said. **"I for sure know that."**

"I'm sure you do, better than most." She patted my hand. "So I have more to thank you for than saving my life. It led to meeting you, and to this trip! And what this trip is doing is reminding me how much I love being a part of life. So, essentially, young lady, you were instrumental in *giving* me back my life!"

I pondered that. I *did* know what it was like to feel on the edges of life. Someone like Miss Gertie could feel that way too? That was a shocker!

"So what are you going to do next with your life?" I dared to ask. I hoped she'd say, *Get back into acting.* But she surprised me.

"Well, I'm seriously considering making a big move after this trip is over."

"To where?"

She waved her slender hand toward the window. "To family. To England."

I gulped. She'd stay here? But then I nodded in understanding. I was feeling a little homesick as well. I missed Penny and Butterscotch, and yes, my parents!

Miss Gertie rubbed my arm. "You won't be rid of me," she added. "I do love Cincinnati summers! Now, missy, are you ready for your big debut at I.D.E.A.?"

"Nope! Not yet. But I will be!" I promised.

I thought about all the good stuff that had happened in my life. And all the bad stuff as well. And you know what? The good manages to overcome the bad every time.

CHAPTER 41

The building that the I.D.E.A. symposium was being held in was probably built when King Arthur was a boy. Or, well, when he would have been a boy if he'd been real. Let's just say, it looked ancient. And had actual turrets. It seriously looked like one of those castles that the Knights of the Round Table might have lived in.

Huge slate-gray stone walls surrounded the place, with a very real-looking gatehouse. The place even had a moat! Okay, actually, it was a small pond that curved halfway around the building, but as long as we're in castle mode, it shall be called a moat!

Mrs. V guided me inside. The entryway had been

hand-painted. Literally, handprints of every color colored the walls. Tiny baby prints, huge grandfather prints, handprints with missing fingers, handprints that looked curled or shriveled or distorted. It reminded me of the day at camp when we made handprints on poster board. But this display felt like captured history, and resilience, and at the same time, kind of felt like the wall itself was waving, beckoning me in.

Then I looked down and saw hundreds of footprints— tiny baby toes as well as stomps of huge feet, some on tiptoe like a ballerina. There were circles that had clearly been left by crutches, and—ooh, the tracks of wheelchairs. "This is quite a welcome," Mrs. V whispered to me. I'll say. What an awesome welcome mat! It made me forget my nerves for a moment.

There was an actual welcoming committee as well. A man with really huge biceps—like weight-lifter arms— but no legs or feet that I could see, sat in a chair and was telling attendees where to sign in.

A teenage girl with a messy bun gave a wave. "I'll take you over!" Mrs. V followed her to a guy about sixteen, who gently bounced as he signed me in and gave us schedules—he was on walking blades. I looked around, wondering if my eyes were as wide as they felt. There were so many kids here! Loads were checking in, some were passing out what looked like agendas or schedules.

But several were like me, using assistive devices. I'm not sure I expected that!

Back at camp, a few of the kids had fancy chairs, but whoa, some of the ones here were state of the art. I hardly knew where to look. One girl's wheelchair made mine look like an antique! It had a real engine, not just a small motor, which spewed orange sparks when she pushed a button.

Two teens were talking in sign, their hands flashing so fast! That's something I could never do.

And I could hardly take my eyes off a guy about eighteen in a maroon bucket hat and Hawaiian shorts, riding in a chair that had huge air-filled tires in the front, with smaller, equally bloated wheels in the back—all bright yellow. He noticed me gaping and rolled over. "It's a beach wheelchair," he told me.

"For real?" I typed.

"Yep. Everything here pretty much came from ideas generated at previous symposiums."

"For REAL???" Jeesh. Use your words, Melody! But I was in awe, and so, ha ha ha, tongue-tied.

"I kid you not. Take a look around! Get inspired!" He flashed a grin, then spun around to greet another newcomer.

Mrs. V was also looking around approvingly. She asked if I felt comfortable, or did I want her to stay. I told her to go go go. She'd mentioned we were near an art gallery called The Tate, and I knew she wanted to see it. So I said it again, go go go. As I did, a girl with shiny, shiny hair strode by. I almost didn't notice her until I saw sparkles. She was using a cane that sparkled every time it tapped the floor: she was blind. Another kid had on a helmet with what looked like electronic eyeballs mounted on top. Then three older teenagers, all in matching aqua wheelchairs, rolled over, the tires looking like those on mountain bikes, but twice as thick with deep grooves in them. Their matching T-shirts boldly said, FACE US AND RACE US. YOU CAN'T OUTPACE US. I laughed.

"Ahmad here came up with this idea two years ago," one of them, a girl, said. "He used to mountain bike before his accident. And now he's mountain-chair-biking!"

"True, all true," Ahmad confirmed. "I got the idea from watching the Paralympics a few years ago, where they had those skiers in wheelchairs with skis welded to the bottom." Ahmad pulsed energy. "I thought that was way cool, and then I thought, why can't I get back on my favorite trails, right?"

"Really cool," I managed to type. Well, at least it was better than "For real"!

A girl with bright green hair joined us. She looked like she had more body control than I did—and her chair was all souped up like a race car. It had turn signals and headlights and even backup lights! She directed its motion with just a touch of a few buttons. So awesome! Goals!

"Hi," the girl said. "I'm Bethany. Have you signed in yet?"

I tapped out, **"Hi! I just did. But I can't stop looking around! Oh, I'm Melody! Sorry! I'm soooo distracted."**

"Yeah, us chair kids are pretty hard to ignore. And if you ignore us, we'll do something to get your attention." Her smile was genuine and confident.

I paused, then tapped, **"I love your hair!"**

She gave it a flounce. "Thanks. I change the color every month—just for fun. It drives my mother crazy!" I loved that she acted like talking to someone on a machine was nothing unusual.

"Everybody here seems pretty extraordinary," I tapped.

Bethany replied, "I specialize in ordinary, except for my hair!"

We both laughed.

"How did you get invited?" I asked, hoping I wasn't being too nosy.

"I invented a way to make peppermints grow on maple trees," she said, smirking.

"For real?" I tapped. OMG, I had to stop typing that!

"You're gonna be fun to hang out with," Bethany said. "You'll believe anything!"

"Okay, you got me this time. Won't happen again," I said, almost a dare.

"Oh, I'm just getting started!" Bethany replied. She held a hand in the air. I grinned and gave her a wobbly high five.

"My turn. How did *you* get invited? Are you famous or something?"

"Not really. I called the emergency folks for the lady next door. No big deal."

"Sounds like a big deal to me! You save her life or something like that?"

"Something like that," I admitted.

"But that's amazing!" she said.

"I guess? But you still haven't told me how you got invited here."

She scratched her nose, a shadow flashing across her face. Then it was gone and the smile was back. "So, I'm a dancer. Jazz, modern, and ballet. Three years ago, I was visiting the States, heading to New York to audition for the Alvin Ailey summer dance program. But we got in a tractor-trailer accident instead."

My face went, *Oh no.*

"Yeah, spinal cord injury. But the top half of me works perfectly."

"So sorry," I tapped.

Her eyes caught mine. "Thanks. But you know, it could have been way worse. And it didn't stop me from dancing."

I typed, **"Question Mark Question Mark Question Mark."**

"Clever. Your computer is so cool!"

"I call her Elvira. So, how do you still dance?"

"I do wheelchair ballet! You give me the right music and my specially modified chair, and I can dance all night!"

"Awesome!"

Bethany paused, then asked, "You ever heard of Stephen Hawking?"

"Sure. Genius physicist who used a talking board like mine."

"Well, it seems to me that the kids who got invited here are the genius kids like he was. Me, I'm just a kid who loves ballet, dyes her hair green, and figured out how to dance with what the world calls a disability. Basically, I don't really know why they invited me!"

Whaaaaat? Bethany had the WHY MEs too? Even though she figured out a way to dance when people probably told her she'd never dance again?

I tapped out. **"That's why you are here. You did something people never imagined you being able to do!"** I gave her my most intense look cuz I was dead serious.

"I guess? What I'd love to do, actually, is make wheel-chair ballet available for chair kids everywhere." She gave me a saucy grin. "Music cures, you know."

"Great goal!" Then I tapped, **"I danced with a boy at summer camp."**

"Oh yeah?" Bethany said. "Was he cute?"

"Very!"

"You still talk to him? What's his name?"

"Sometimes. Online. Noah. He makes me smile."

And there I was—smiling at the thought of Noah, and fireflies, and starlight. He would've been so into all the energy here.

A bell rang in the distance. It was followed by a chime, then a buzzer, then a drumming sound. When I looked around quizzically, Bethany told me that they used different sounds to make sure everyone could hear.

She pulled out the schedule. "Sooo, looks like first we go to the auditorium for the 'informational opening.'" Bethany made air quotes.

Yeah, "informational opening" sounded kinda boring. But nothing about this had been boring so far, so I rolled in the direction a stream of other kids were headed, Bethany rolling beside me.

CHAPTER 42

The emcee was a woman with shoulder-length hair white as snow—her dress long, flowing, and dark purple—who strode over to the auditorium's podium, her arms opened wide. Behind her was a screen projecting closed-captioning.

"Hello, people! Welcome to London!" she boomed out while her hands seemed to dance as she simultaneously signed, the words near instantly projecting onto the screen. "Welcome to the twentieth session of the I.D.E.A. symposium. Can you believe that we have over a hundred teen guests from seventeen countries here with us this year? Wonderful! And a special welcome to Sri

Lanka!" Two kids hooted from the back. "You're the first to visit from your beautiful country." She looked around the room, seeming to see every one of us. "I'm your host, Charlene Chilvers, and I'm thrilled to welcome you *all* to this year's International Society of Innovation, Discovery, Energy, and Application. Yep, I.D.E.A. Because we have the ideas that will change the world! In fact, ha-ha, one idea from your predecessors was to shorten the definition to 'I'm Doing It All'—love it!" She paused as cheers and stomps and hollers followed.

"Now, you've all been summoned here, no, not by one of our resident wizards—this *was* a castle, you know—but because your achievements; your promise; your strength; and, equally important, your ingenuity.

"All of you have demonstrated capabilities to see the world through a unique lens, and that, my friends—and I can promise you that by the time we leave here, we will all be friends—is the key to innovation and invention. You've all shown a desire to help others, which is the best type of motivation. And that's why, while we will be celebrating differences and listening to each other's stories, our focus for the past two decades has always been on how to make life better, easier, more hospitable, for others. For one person, for legions.

"Now, I need to get off this stage so you lovely people can see what your brains and hearts can achieve unfettered, and with like-hearted people. So I'll wrap my welcome up by saying, go over your schedules carefully. If you didn't get one already, go to the sign-in area— we have them in all of your native languages, as well as Braille. You'll see a vast variety of workshops, classes, and demonstrations, as well as lots of really good food! If you're here from 'across the pond,' we want your visit to Great Britain to be the most personally rewarding experience of your lives. And if you have any questions or problems, please reach out to anyone on our staff. You can't miss us—we're the only ones dressed in purple!"

Purple? I hadn't even noticed!

"Okay. Ready to start the day?" she called out. A roar of "YES" answered, accompanied by squawks from kids like me, and clangs from someone who had cowbells, and a jangle of a tambourine. *Great way to make yourself heard,* I thought appreciatively.

"Excellent," Ms. Chilvers said. "Now repeat after me: We are WORLD CHANGERS! Louder! WE ARE WORLD CHANGERS! WE ARE WORLD CHANGERS! And we have the IDEAS to change the world for the better."

I found myself shouting those words in my head, over and over. I felt strong, powerful, and READY. For what, exactly, I didn't quite know. But I knew I would, eventually, and I'd be ready for it!

• • • •

As people streamed out of the auditorium, Bethany and I stayed behind a moment. She propped the schedule on my board—there were so many choices! Talks on latest trends in philanthropy. Talks on areas in society with unexpected needs. Workshops helping people become better advocates. Others on affordability and how to find "angels"—people who would sponsor big projects, or help you network to get the support for your vision. The list went on and on.

I definitely wanted to hear about how to become a better advocate, and they had a morning session. Great!

But the one that I was most psyched about was the innovation workshop, where you brainstormed ideas that would improve people's lives. Bethany and I huddled over the schedule.

"It's three hours long," she read. "Seems super popular; they have three different sessions!"

I squinted at the page. **"One this afternoon!"**

"Oh, and check this out . . . one of the innovation workshops is set up for kids who need translators. This place thinks of everything!" Bethany sat up straight. "Let's sign up quick, before all those sessions get filled!" She wanted to do that one too! Psych!

I suggested that we should sign up for the afternoon session first, as that way we'd definitely get a slot, figuring most kids would sign up in order, morning first, then afternoon.

"Quite the strategist, you," Bethany said, high-fiving me as we secured the workshop. This morning she wanted to hear about the "angels," since it might help with the wheelchair dance program she'd been dreaming about. I was most interested in the advocacy session. We agreed to meet up for lunch. Rolling over there, seeing all the other kids bombing around, made me wonder what school would have been like if it were more like this—where you felt the opposite of excluded: wanted, needed!

The session was packed. The guy I was sitting beside, several years older than me, leaned over to say, "Our lecturer's from Oxford—he has so many PhDs and honors I can't remember half of them, and I remember literally everything."

"Photographic memory?" I typed.

He nodded. "A blessing and a curse. Sometimes I feel like I play air traffic control with my own brain to get the right info down!"

Huh, I never thought of it that way. And the lecturer, who you'd think would have been about ninety because of all his degrees, was only in his thirties. He said his "jam" was public policy and how to work within it to make change. He talked about how to find the right people to talk to. How to create effective emails and properly position requests or concerns. How to convince people to rally to your cause to support it. Then he had a few other people come in—some telling us about things they'd accomplished and how they'd made that happen. It was fascinating. And inspiring! My mind was already churning, locking in the information. I was having Elvira record it, too, so I could listen again later!

CHAPTER 43

Mrs. V arrived exactly at lunchtime. She helped me with a quick trip to the restroom, which was the best-equipped bathroom in the universe—even better than the ones we had at camp! Each stall had bars and straps and even a system that automatically helped a person from their wheelchair to the toilet and back again.

As we came out, I saw Bethany leaving her session. I waved and introduced Mrs. V, who was totally into Bethany's hair and wondered how her own graying brown curls would look green. Boxed lunches, everyone's labeled for anyone with special—or mushy—diets, like mine, were being passed out at long tables near the wall of hands. Mrs. V collected my box, then suggested eating outside. "When do you get to have a picnic by a "moat"? We're blessed with another gorgeous day. I hope we don't use up London's yearly allotment of them!"

"Seriously!" Bethany agreed.

"I thought it rained here all the time," I tapped.

"Shhhh. Don't remind the skies! Let's just enjoy it."

We both laughed, and sat under a weeping willow that swayed above us. Noisy ducks paddled nearby.

"We have blue jays in the yard next door," I tapped. **"I watch them from my window."**

"They're so pretty. I've seen a few of them up in Yorkshire, where I'm from, but they're rather rare," Bethany said. "But we've got falcons! You can train them to carry messages, and they can fly for hundreds of miles."

"Falcons are boss. I read that medieval kings had them. Must be hard to train a bird for war!"

"Couldn't wear armor! It'd never get off the ground!" Bethany said with a giggle. Odd, for some reason, "never get off the ground" struck me. Made me think of Miss Gertie and her fall. I shook the thought away. Miss Gertie had not only gotten off the ground, she flew to London!

Mrs. V spooned me the last bite of cottage pie, which, seriously, I was hoping Mom could find the recipe for, because it was YUM. My thoughts drifted toward that "moat" and how moats kept buildings and the people in them safe. But did the folks who lived way back then ever feel trapped? Because a moat could work both ways, keeping others out, but keeping you in.

And then I found myself thinking about Miss Gertie again. . . . She'd sort of trapped herself in, well, herself for a long time, not letting anyone (or anyone's pie!) in. She stayed nice and safe—and I got that!—but she'd isolated herself too. And so when she fell, she didn't have anyone close to her who would have noticed and helped. If I hadn't been looking at that dreary rain and pooping blue jay . . . Hmm, in keeping herself too safe, in some ways she'd become unsafe. We all need each other, I was thinking.

And at that moment came the chimes, bells, and drums we'd heard earlier. Lunch was over. Bethany pulled her hair into a quick ponytail.

"Gearing up for the next session?" I typed.

She mimed some jazz movements with her arms. "Ready to rock and roll!"

CHAPTER 44

I waved hello to the painted hands as we rolled back in as Mrs. V waved goodbye, saying she'd pick me up at five o'clock.

"We get to add our handprints up there on the last day," Bethany told me. "I think I need to go green, to match my hair." I was thinking, *That's a great custom. What color would I choose?* But I didn't have time to decide now; we had to get to our workshop.

The room where the workshop took place was a hexagon, its ornately carved wood burnished. Tapestries hung high on each wall depicted various scenes of unicorns and lions coexisting with gowned ladies in tall pointed hats. How the heck long did it take to make those? I wondered. Before each wall sat a table facing the room's center, pads of paper stacked on each corner. The leader waved us in like she was hailing a cab. Six other teens were already seated, and two more came in right after us. They were loud and excited, talking about the hydraulics used in something they'd seen when they'd first arrived.

The leader, her bright dark-brown eyes taking us all in, leaned against one of the tables. "Based on the energy I'm already feeling in this room," she began, "I can tell that at least one thing that's never existed before will exist, at least in idea form, by the end of this session."

"Oh yeah!" one of the guys said with a fist pump. We all nodded excitedly.

"Oh YEAH!" the woman repeated, standing tall. "I'm Audrey Watkins, but feel free to call me Audrey. I've been running this workshop for the past five years, and it's never ended without a good idea."

First she had us introduce ourselves and say where we were from. One guy with closely cropped hair was here from Ukraine. Another guy whose hair flopped down into his face was from Peru. And a stunningly beautiful girl with short-cropped hair had flown in from South Africa. A girl from Malaysia in really hip, funky clothes—a fellow thrifter?—drummed her pencil on a pad she had already scooped up; she was ready to GO!

Audrey quickly gave a rundown of the session. First we would brainstorm a slew of ideas, then we'd all get together to zero in on the ones we decided were strongest and collectively develop them further. It all sounded fab, until she announced that tomorrow, at the symposium roundup, we would be giving a quick speech about our inventions and the philosophies behind them.

Wait, did she say a speech? We had to give a speech? I swung round to Bethany. But of course she had no idea what was going on in my mind. Sky would have in a sec. Mrs. V, too. But no way was I going to type out my panic to everyone in this room, all older than me. I was already feeling like an imposter.

Audrey felt the energy of the room shift, and quickly let us know that the speech wasn't mandatory. *Okay, Melody, calm yourself, girl.* I replayed what Audrey had said, my breathing returning to normal. There was a "not mandatory" in there. Right! Okay, so I didn't HAVE to give a speech. Once again I was grateful for my seat belt, as I was about to slide right out of the chair in relief.

Audrey listed several of the previous year's ideas, some of which had actually come to fruition. "You probably saw several when you walked in," she said proudly. "But you don't have to think grandiose . . . as long as it is beneficial to someone in our world, it's worthy!" I liked that a lot.

"Saving the world one day at a time," I ventured, Elvira's voice on low, low, low. Bethany and the two guys at the closest table gave *you got that right* nods.

We had an hour to brainstorm, then we'd read our ideas to each other and see what stuck. Audrey offered to take notes for anyone who needed help, but we were all good. I typed papers for school all the time on my board. I was on it!

At first we all kind of looked at each other. Everyone was so quiet, even the loud ones. Audrey let out a laugh. "This isn't a test! Think of yourselves as a teen *Shark Tank*, except you get to play both roles—coming up with ideas, then figuring out the most viable. That way, ha ha ha, no one gets eaten!"

That broke the ice, and whispering began. Which rose to chattering. Which peaked at the occasional shouts of "Ooh, ooh, I've got an even better idea" and "Dang, that wouldn't work, now that I think about it." Balls of paper gathered on tables. One girl just kept flinging her rejects at a wastebasket across the room, and missed every time. A guy had about twenty crumpled balls with five minutes to go, and spent the last five minutes constructing a near-perfect pyramid out of them. Bethany chewed on a chunk of green hair that had slipped free from her ponytail. Now I knew why she pulled it back in the first place; she was a hair chomper! Weird, I'd never thought of that before—I couldn't chomp my fingernails or my hair.

In case you're wondering, the reason why I had so much time to watch everyone else was because at first I was coming up with ideas that were—sorry, Audrey— bad! So bad I didn't spend more than a few minutes on them. Like, somehow the first thing that popped into my head was moving sidewalks, kind of like the ones I'd seen at the airport. That would sure help people who had trouble walking. But yeah, changing all the sidewalks in the world to moving ones? Never going to happen! I would have loved the feeling of crumpling up a piece of paper and giving it a toss, but I had to be satisfied with Elvira's delete button.

I looked out the window, contemplating the latest probably bad idea, thinking how lucky I was to be here, even with my bad ideas. I wasn't in idea panic mode yet. I wondered whether Sky was having a good time with her relatives in Bath. A bird flitted by the window—the windows here had these laced metal bands crossing them, instead of regular windowpanes. The bird circled back, landed on the outside sill, pecked at something, then off it went. It looked bluish, but I couldn't quite tell. And then I was thinking of Mrs. V's blue jays and the poopy window, and then I was thinking of that poopy window morning and then I was thinking of Miss Gertie . . . Miss Gertie!

And BOOM. I had my idea. I typed it in. I typed some notes about it. I hit save. I hit save again in case the first save didn't save! And I watched basketball girl clap her hands together, a piece of paper finally staying flat on her desk, her marker down. She saw me watching and gave me a thumbs-up. I smiled hard and hoped she knew that meant a thumbs-up back.

CHAPTER 45

Brains fascinate me. You never know what anyone's brain is going to come up with. And everyone, every single ding-dang person in the universe, has a completely different brain. And what's completely bananas to think about is that everyone, e-v-e-r-y-o-n-e, is pretty much always thinking, and everyone's thoughts are different from everyone else's. I'm talking EIGHT BILLION PEOPLE! Unless they're sleeping. And even then their brains are thinking, because aren't dreams a type of thought? I thought so. Ha. But! If everyone is thinking something a bunch of times a day, times eight billion people, even if people had, say, twenty thoughts per day, that would

be 160 billion thoughts. A day! And probably there were way more thoughts than twenty per day per person! My brain was exploding! Stephen Hawking, where are you?!

Why was I thinking all this? Because I was already in awe of the ideas that my workshop crew had come up with, which all came from thoughts. Audrey had us shimmy our tables closer to the center for the idea-palooza, she called it. The first guy to share his ideas—Akihiko—was so shy and soft-spoken I immediately guessed that he chose to go first to get it over with and not sit there feeling even *more* nervous. Excellent tactic. He had three ideas; we liked the one for lighter, smaller, kid-friendly noise-cancelling headphones for toddlers who got sensory overload the best. Basketball girl, like me, had only one idea that she wanted to share, but she was mega excited about it. Something about permanent internet connections that could, like, supersonically click in when you went out of range, anywhere. Two guys—Aengus, from Ireland, and Anders, who I at first thought was Irish because of his red hair (jeesh, never assume, because he was from Sweden, where I thought everyone was blonde. Wow, I really had to stop with the stereotypes!)—had banded together as a team. They were fake-arguing over who would tell their idea.

"Bruh, I came up with it first, so I get to tell it," the freckled, red-hair-to-his-shoulders guy said.

"Uh, yeah, but it was a bloody rotter until *I* saw its

true potential," the other guy countered, yanking at the neck of his T-shirt. The girl at the next table snatched the paper off their table and announced that *she* would read it. Everyone laughed.

Bethany had a pair of ideas, the best having to do with developing a way to enable a wheelchair to slide rather than roll. Yep, she had dance on the brain! I nodded a yes to her, and she shimmied in her seat.

I didn't want to be last, so I quickly typed, **"I'll go next."** Usually I feel kinda (or a lot!) awkward when I have to use Elvira in front of a lot of people around my age—weird, right? I was fine on television, apparently. Groups of kids I don't know, though, nuh-uh. Too judgy. But here, I didn't feel that way at all.

I didn't need to look at my double-saved notes, just started typing as quickly as I could.

"People like me, or elderly people, or people with epilepsy, are often at risk of falling," I typed. Gosh, it took so long to type so little sometimes! But I kept going. **"If you are knocked unconscious, you can't call for help. And your life might be on the line."** I glanced around—everyone looked interested, eager to hear what I would say next. **"I'd like people who need it to have an alert necklace they can wear that goes off only if they fall and can't move."** I paused; my thumb was aching! My leg kicked out. Let me finish, leg!

"Take your time, Melody," Audrey assured me.

The T-shirt guy added props: "Yeah, good ideas can't be rushed!"

I nodded. Typed and typed and typed. **"It calls 911 and sends them your location if it senses no movement after a few seconds. But also sends out a sound as loud as a siren. Outside or inside, anyone nearby can hear it. And help can come more quickly."** My arm swung away from my board. Can just an arm be exhausted? Mine was!

There was a lot of back-and-forth after that. What was so cool was that everyone was into at least one idea that someone else had thought of. And everyone was just as into workshopping everyone else's ideas as they were their own. Basketball girl suggested to Bethany that maybe attaching something like skis, but with lots of small metal balls sitting underneath, could be a way to get a wheelchair to slide. . . .

"Like Heelys," the shy guy chimed in. Quiet but quick, that guy!

The duo guys had great thoughts, one of which was to develop a system so that every single store in England had a setup where you donate one penny each time you bought something, and that money went into a fund that was distributed to people in poverty, so it became a regular thing. Think of how many people could be helped!

"There are over three hundred thousand stores in

the UK," the curly haired duo guy explained. "Quick math and averaging thirty people a day at a shop gets you literally over ninety thousand pounds a day in fund-raising across the country."

"Bruh!" the louder duo guys shouted excitedly. "Get the store to match each penny, and you've got more than one hundred and eighty thousand quid!" I also now knew that "quid" was sort of like an American dollar. Yeah, I was nearly native-born at this point!

"That's over sixty-five MILLION quid a year!"

"Imagine what that could do," Bethany murmured.

Audrey walked from table to table, arms folded, nodding, looking VERY pleased. She was letting us go, and we WENT.

When it got to the point where we'd started talking off topic, she could tell we'd . . . gone. Ha. Our brains were heading toward shutdown mode. Near magically, snacks appeared, and miraculously (to me!), there was a special one for me. "Sticky toffee pudding," Audrey said, laying it in front of me. Ohhh, I couldn't wait to try that!

"Thank you—I'll eat mine after the session" is what I typed. In truth, I might be bold, but asking someone I barely knew to help me eat was not happening! Plus, I was too jazzed up. I wanted to do workshops like this every day!

I was so hyped that I'd forgotten about what Audrey

had said early on. Giving a talk. Once everyone else was re-energized with Twisters (where ice cream and Popsicle swirled around each other, and the Popsicle part was apparently pear!), and Ribena Lollies (basically Popsicles made from black currant juice), Audrey called for our attention.

"All of these phenomenal ideas will be given serious deliberation beyond this weekend, but I'd bet a lot of attendees would love to hear what you all have so brilliantly come up with." She gave us each a You're Brilliant and You're Brilliant and You're Brilliant nod, which made me giggle. My mom loved watching Oprah, and it was like when Oprah said, "And you get a car! And you get a car! And you get a car!"

"As I said, this isn't mandatory. But it's much more impactful if the actual person with the idea shares it. It feels so much more . . . real, I suppose would be the ideal word."

"On it!" shouted the duo boys, who then elbowed each other. As others responded, my insides were quivering. My brain was sparking, not in a good way. Give a speech? In front of everyone at this symposium? Me, who can't talk, give a TALK? Nope. No way.

Bethany was saying, "Certainly!" I was thinking, *Certainly NOT.*

Basketball girl said, "I'm in!" I was thinking, *I'm OUT.*

Shy guy was staring hard at the table, like kids do when they don't want to be called on in class. The word "class" made me suddenly remember the advocacy panel I'd just attended this morning. How the heck was I going to advocate for someone else if I couldn't even advocate for my own idea? I thought back to what Mom had said when this all started—that people like me don't often get a platform like this. But there were soooooooooo many people here. And they'd all hear Elvira. Which did *not* sound like Beyoncé. Which made me think, oof, I should have brought up my personalized voice idea! Which made me think, *Hey, I have a lot of ideas.* And if I didn't talk about them, they were just going to stay ideas. You can't just think, you have to *do.* Okay, brain, talking to me, making all kinds of sense. I'll do it. I'll get my brave on. How? No idea.

My WHY ME had become HOW CAN I?

CHAPTER 46

When we got back to the hotel, I was wiped. But not so wiped that I couldn't eat that sticky toffee pudding, which, by the way, was majorly delicious. I told Mrs. V all about my day in the taxi. Mrs. V told me about everything she saw at the museum—including a gallery of fashion from the 1800s and 1900s from around the world, which she thought I'd love. We'd try to fit it into our last few days after the conference. And she'd walked through a park that led to another palace, called Kensington. Lots of swans there too, she said.

Sky and Miss Gertie weren't going to be back for a few hours, so Mrs. V ordered a creamy potato soup, and my new addiction, mushy peas, for dinner. Full, washed, teeth brushed, my favorite jammies on and in bed, I was all set to focus. I motioned for Elvira. Mrs. V handed it to me.

"Texting your parents?" she asked. "Or special friends?" I knew she meant Noah. I grunted, and began to type.

"I need to give a talk. In front of EVERYONE."

"Ah, but that's exciting! About the idea you came up with? Which, I can't emphasize this enough, is a wonderful, thoughtful idea, Melody." She brushed a hand over my head. "My heart fills just thinking about it! And one day, when I'm older, I might *need* it. So your timing is excellent."

"Funny! But how can I give a speech?! All those people!"

"Well, you've written dozens of papers for school. Writing a talk is just like that—just think about what you want people to know, break it down into an order from one thing to the next, like a ladder, and end with something that gets people motivated, excited."

I gave a squawk-squeal and typed, **"You make it sound so easy."**

"I'm just saying it's a lot less difficult if you think of it in sections. You have a wonderful way with words. Trust that."

Welp, I didn't have much choice. I wondered if it was easier or harder to give a speech using a board. Maybe creating the speech was easier, because I could type it up ahead of time. And giving it was easier too, because Elvira would say it for me. Sure wish I had a Beyoncé voice on that machine. Or even Ian's from Double Trouble! That would be so cool. My thoughts flitted over to *Oohhhh, we were going to go see them record in their studio once the symposium was over!* Was it scary for them to play a new song for the first time? Then my brain yelled, *Melody! Focus! Okay, back to the speech.* What to say, that was the hardest part. Or maybe being up there in front of everyone would be harder. I wouldn't know until I did it. And I couldn't do it until I started.

An hour later, I wasn't even halfway through! My thumb was probably getting a blister on a blister. And I couldn't focus. Talking about the rescue device was easy. But tying it into why I was at the symposium, and how I was inspired to think of my idea, was sooooo much harder. I flung myself back against the mountain of pillows Mrs. V had piled behind me to keep me propped up.

She looked over from whatever she was watching on TV. "Honestly, how did I not know about this show?" she asked. "And what's with you, missy? You've been typing so much I thought you were writing a novel!"

"I wish. This is HARD."

"Melody, what did we talk about the other day? You were chosen to be here. Everyone loved your idea.

You're here because they want to hear from you. Or else
they would have chosen some other exceptional young
person." Mrs. V was great at giving pep talks, but it wasn't
working. My brain wasn't saying, *You were chosen*. It was
begging and pleading to go to sleep.

I didn't HAVE to do it. Did I have to do it? I mean,
what was Audrey going to do if I changed my mind? I bet
kids had bailed out before. That was it. I'd tell her in the
morning. I felt instantly relieved.

But then I thought of the shy boy. Audrey was asking
about who'd talk about their idea. He'd kept his head
down the whole time, until I had told Audrey yes. That
was when he finally looked up and said he'd do it too.

Shoot! Would it be rotten not to do it when it seemed
like my doing it was what helped convince him to as well?
Sooo, maybe my words did make a difference, if only to
him? GAHHHHHHHH.

"Uh, Melody, you okay?" I almost jumped, I was so in
my head. "You've been grunting and humming away as
if you're arguing with yourself!" Mrs. V said.

I waved an arm, then tapped out, **"I was."**

"Well, who won?"

"Me!"

By the time Sky (her new turquoise spikes looking awesome) and Miss Gertie got back, full of news about the

town they'd visited and the lake they'd seen and the Roman baths that Sky was geeking out about, telling me that they have been there since 60 AD!, I'd finished a rough draft of something that might be a speech kind of thing. Once I'd stopped feeling all uptight, I started to think about why I'd been chosen, and how that led to my idea. I thought about all the support I'd been given all my life, and how every bit gave me more and more power to be more . . . me. I thought about how much I had to give, how much I could do, how I'd learned I had every right to have dreams, and how everyone else did too. And how I wanted to think beyond my own dreams to bigger ones, to help others have a chance to dream. And then I thought, I HOPED, I knew what to say. I might read it over in the morning and decide I was really, truly going to jump ship! No promises. But at least the speech was written.

CHAPTER 47

Mrs. V, at seven o'clock the next morning, was dancing with a dress. What? Was I still asleep? I shook my head to clear it. Nope. She was doing some sad, sad, sad-looking waltz-like thing, with a dusty blue capped-sleeve sundress.

"Melodyyyyyyyy," she sang out. She one-two-three'd, one-two-three'd over to me. I couldn't even ask her, *What the heck?* as I didn't have my board yet! But Mrs. V anticipated my tapping.

"I got this for you while I was out and about yesterday— I figured you'd want something nice to wear for the close of the symposium!" Man, Mrs. V has to be one of the most thoughtful people alive! She held it out so I could touch it. It was supercute, made of a silky, flowy material, long to cover my knobby knees. It cinched at the waist with a navy sash. It was perfect.

Mrs. V handed me my board. **"I can wear my black boots with it!"** I tapped.

"How about your sandals?" Mrs. V suggested.

"Black boots!" a voice chimed in from under a pillow. Did I tell you Sky slept with her pillow ON her head?

I laughed. **"Love this dress! Thank you so much! To prove it, I'll wear the sandals."** They both laughed.

Before we all left for I.D.E.A., I had Sky read over my speech. I didn't want to sound like a little kid. She was blinking hard by the time she was done.

"Is it so bad you're crying?" I joked, feeling nervous.

"I'm not crying! I don't cry! Okay, sometimes I do. Okay, maybe I got a little . . . misty." Then she gave me a hug. "This is pure power, you know? And I think you could end up being a speechwriter for the president."

"Really?"

"Truly!"

Day two of the I.D.E.A. symposium was just as interesting as the first, and since we'd taken the most intense workshop yesterday, a little less intense. Mrs. V and Miss Gertie and Sky headed off to do some more sightseeing but would meet me once the workshops and talks were over.

I searched out Bethany immediately, and the duo boys jogged over as well. They even said they liked my dress. Bethany was wearing a sundress too! I waved Shy Boy toward us. We chose a silly-sounding assembly for our first session. It was simply called "Be Loud." Ha. Most of the time kids are told to "Be Quiet." We had to check this out. And yep, it was LOUD.

First, the man in charge—Mr. Vora, who was with the London Symphony—had us humming. Then mooing! Then roaring! Then yelling. Then screaming. Whoa, could I scream. Everyone's faces got beet red, and we all started laughing at each other. I hope no random tourists were walking outside—they'd think knights were slaughtering us! Seems most people don't make use of how LOUD they can be, and it can be really "cathartic"— you kind of go vocally crazy, and when you're done, you feel, weirdly, very calm. True, that!

Next we were each given a noisemaker of some sort—a bell, a whistle, a thunder stick, a horn, a kazoo, a shaker, a drum—and lots of others. I was given two bracelets full of dozens of golden bells, one for each wrist. And then Mr. Vora had us follow rhythms he played for us on his phone with our noisemaker. The first sounded sort of like a musically mixed-up nursery rhyme. The next had an Indian cadence, and the next, an American Indian beat. Mexican, Nigerian, Spanish, German, Chinese. Some I didn't recognize. It was so fun. A room full of forty teenagers, all having fun with instruments.

But then Mr. Vora did the most unexpected thing. He divided us into groups, one for each type of rhythm. He had us practice our assigned rhythm for about two minutes. And once we all had our rhythms down, he pulled out his phone and tapped a few times.

"Okay, everyone. On the count of three, play your assigned rhythms."

We did, and it sounded like . . . like nothing I'd ever heard before in my whole entire life. It gave me shivers. When we finished, Mr. Vora shouted, "Again." So we did it again, every head turning, trying to grasp and understand what we were hearing.

"And one more time!"

One more time? Heck, I wanted to do this for the rest of the day. Mr. Vora finally turned off his phone. He wove in and out among us, clapping slowly, deliberately. Everyone looked as puzzled as I was.

Once he'd circled back to the front of the room, he picked up his phone again. Tapped it a few times, laid it on the podium. And out burst exactly what we'd been playing—all our rhythms, but we were listening to them as a whole.

"Who can tell me what this sounds like?" he asked, hands on his hips. More looking around.

"Beautiful noise?" ventured one girl.

"Controlled chaos!" yelled the red-haired duo boy.

Mr. Vora was nodding. "All valid guesses. But can anyone go further afield?"

An idea was coming to me. I caught the eye of Shy Boy. His eyes were sparking. He had an idea too. I nodded to him, hoping it was a *you go first* head nod, as my nods can sometimes look like wobbles. He gave a sweet smile and said, "It sounds to me like . . . hearing the whole world, simultaneously."

I thought Mr. Vora was going to leap over us all to hug Shy Boy, he looked so pleased. *Whoa.* Guess that was the right answer.

And I guess this was one of the best classes I'd ever taken.

Sky surprised me by meeting me for lunch, which was fab, because I got to introduce her to Bethany and a few of the others. We picked up more gourmet boxed lunches, and went out to "our place," as Bethany called it, under the weeping willow. At this point, I wasn't even embarrassed to eat in front of the others. We laughed and joked and the T-shirt duo boy—Aengus—said he'd seen a beanbag toss, so he hopped up to get it. You honestly can't imagine how bad I am at beanbag toss! But I don't know when I ever laughed so hard. I had to make myself stop so I wouldn't have an accident in my new dress. Red-haired duo guy—Anders—was at a Beanbag Olympics level. So were Sky and Bethany. Then the game was down to Sky and Anders; he had this very elaborate pull-back before he let the beanbag fly at the hole. Sky was sleek, one fluid motion, and I noticed she was wearing . . . my boots! She and Anders were completely tied, the rest of us rooting for both of them, but I noticed Aengus rooting a little harder for Sky. Oooooo! Then came that chiming, pinging, tinkling bell ring.

"Saved by the bell!" Shy Boy—Akihiko—said with a laugh.

"Saved by the bell!" we all shouted. Well, I shouted it in my head, but that counts!

For the afternoon session, those of us who'd done the innovation workshops were asked to a special session. It was to explain our ideas to a group of adults who came from all sorts of backgrounds. Mechanical engineers. Chemists. Welders. A sound technician. Finance guys, none wearing business suits, as it was way too warm out. The head of some big department store conglomerate. Even a dance instructor! They asked so many questions and nodded so often *they* could have been bobbleheads. They took us seriously, really seriously, was what I noticed the most. We were offering our best ideas, and they mattered to these folks.

I was glad we were so busy—it kept me from worrying about the speech part of the day. During a break, I went with Bethany to add our handprints to the wall. She chose green, while I chose—take a guess!—yep, royal blue. I love knowing my hands will be there long after I'm gone. I will always be a part of this place, and my hands will be there to welcome next year's teens!

But all of a sudden, it was time. I saw Mrs. V, Sky, and Miss Gertie being ushered over to the observers' area to be seated, along with a lot of other adults, clearly many of them parents. The I.D.E.A. kids who weren't participating in the final presentation filed in as well. All of us innovation workshop kids were seated on the sides, so we could easily get up to the stage when it was our turn.

I gulped. There were a lot of people out there!

Ms. Chilvers took the stage, the backdrop behind her a kaleidoscope of images—previous years' groups, inventions, powerful sayings—intermingled with an image of the hands that welcomed us in at the entryway of the building. I liked how that was what tied everything together, those hands. To me the hands meant we were all together in this, in this life. And dreams mattered, and *ideas* mattered, but what mattered more was to work together to make dreams actually happen. I wanted to tell Bethany this, but Elvira didn't do whisper.

Ms. Chilvers looked amazing—she'd had her hair done in bouncy waves and had changed from her purple outfit to a trendy all-pink pantsuit with a ruffly white blouse. I giggled as I thought of a good description for it: Power Pretty! She'd really gone all out, with pink lipstick, too, and high-heeled espadrilles. She welcomed everyone, gave a shorter version of her opening speech, I guess for the parents and guests, then called all the lecturers and advisors to the stage for a round of applause, signing the entire time. We kids all hooted and hollered, way more fun than clapping.

She started talking about inspiration, then cut herself off. "I'm a big believer in show me, don't tell me. So I want you all to meet a previous I.D.E.A. attendee, who can *show* you far more eloquently than I can *tell* you."

And onto the stage rode a guy I hadn't seen before. Bethany gave me a quick nudge, because, okay, he was cute as heck. And definitely not shy!

He reached the center of the stage and belted out, "Hey, all. My name is Ukiah. I am proudly from the Native American Pomo tribe, and my name means 'deep valley.' I first came to I.D.E.A. three years ago, and I have power!" He pressed a knob on the side of his chair, and it began to rise and rise, until he was the same height as a standing adult! How great was that? I had no idea such a thing existed.

"I didn't like always feeling below people, or people having to squat to talk to me. Made me mad," Ukiah continued. "So I decided to do something about it instead of complaining or feeling bad. I channeled that mad into inspiration—an idea. And this is what I came up with—a chair with a power lift and a power motor. I can also do wheelies in this thing—when it's down. But when I forget to plug it into the electric socket, I got nothing!"

The audience laughed. "So people," he finished up, "I'm glad to be here to tell all of you, and the rest of the world as well, that we *all* have power. We just have to do something with it." And with that, he lowered his chair and left the stage, doing a wheelie!

Everybody in the crowd hooted or drummed or whistled as Ukiah made his way back into the audience.

A few more kids from previous years came on to talk about or show what they accomplished or changed since attending the symposium. One girl, in college now, had been the first person to come up with the idea for special glare-reducing glasses to wear for driving at night. She said most car accidents happen at night, and sometimes it's because the glare from headlights of an approaching car makes it hard to see. Her inspiration came from almost losing her brother in a nighttime accident. *Wow, how many people are alive today because of her?* I thought.

A boy who looked about Sky's age sauntered onto the stage next and flashed us all a peace sign. After quickly signing with Ms. Chilvers, he took her place behind the podium to explain, in sign, how he'd created a computer program that instantly translated someone's sign into words—that was how the screen behind him was able to capture in words everything he was telling us! He triumphantly held up an iPad, which had been sitting on the podium, like a trophy. More raucous clapping followed.

At this point, Ms. Chilvers was practically shimmering with excitement. She went up to the mic again, and was literally bouncing on her toes. "And now for one of my favorite parts of the program! We get to hear from this year's incredibly forward-thinking young people, who will tell you about their ideas . . . for the future!"

She paused, and looked around dramatically. "We always invite a guest presenter for this portion, and as you'd read, this year it was to be the head of British Aerospace. Unfortunately, he was called out of the country."

She allowed for a moment of "Awwws" and "That's a right shame." Oddly, Ms. Chilvers looked delighted about this. She broke out into a tremendous smile, flipped her hair from her shoulders, and announced, "But hearing of our dilemma, an extra-special guest decided to step in. Someone for whom innovation and forward thinking is a hallmark." Again she paused. So dramatic, this woman!

Squaring her shoulders, she at last announced, "It is my enormous honor to introduce you to His Royal Highness Prince William!"

CHAPTER 48

I truly, utterly froze. Prince William? Here? Bethany whacked her elbow into mine on one side and Anders elbowed me on the other. But all I could do was stare. Probably my mouth was wide open. I didn't care. A real live prince was walking across the stage. He was so tall! His legs were so long it only took him about five strides. He had on a crisp navy linen suit and a periwinkle-blue tie, a silk handkerchief in the top pocket of his jacket. His eyes were as bright as the tie. And can a nose look regal? Whatever. His did. A prince was here. On a stage. Right in front of us.

Everyone jumped to their feet (well, nearly everyone,

ha). The clapping was a roar. Some of the guys finger-whistled, the sound cracking above the clapping, sounding like fiery orange. Ms. Chilvers was blushing as pink as her power suit.

The prince adjusted his necktie and smiled that type of small smile you do when you're really, really happy but don't want to be cheesing. He waited so long for the clapping to die down that he finally had to pat at the air in a quiet-down-folks manner. Clearly everyone else was as surprised as I was.

"I'm awfully glad to be here with you this afternoon," he began in a very posh accent. "You might not know this, but I'm an idea junkie." He grinned out at us. "I've always been drawn to think tanks. In fact, I've brought a number of them under the Prince's Trust, as I find them terribly inspirational and am thus compelled to support them as much as I'm able. Because our futures are at stake! And in this arena, little impresses me more than hearing ideas from the very people—you idea makers—whose futures will be most impacted by what can come out of programs like these."

He smiled broadly, looking out at us, taking his time—I'm sure all of us felt the power of his gaze. "The royal family is full of tradition, but I see it as the foundation for the future, as well. By supporting programs like I.D.E.A., we're committing to helping make dreams for the future become realities. We take what we've learned in the past and use it to power the thoughts for tomorrow, just as you have done this very weekend.

"But enough from me; I'm sure you're all as eager as I am to hear what our future might hold." He gave a cheeky smirk and added, one hand cupped by his mouth, "I do love a sneak peek!" And he waved up at the first speaker.

For the first few presentations, I could hardly focus on what my fellow workshoppers were saying because I was getting more and more nervous. What if Elvira broke down? Had I even charged her? I couldn't remember! What if the sound connection didn't connect? What if I, OMG, kicked the prince?!

Akihiko went up next. I don't know if he'd practiced all night, but he nailed it, and he owned it. Prince William was looking so intent, so there, so . . . in the moment. This was important to him. Our ideas were important to him. The prince actually walked right over to Akihiko, clapping just for him, and then slipped a lanyard over his head. I was curious enough about what was on it to forget my what-ifs for a hot minute.

But after Akihiko came Anders and Aengus. And after them would be . . . nope. No, no, no, I was not going to get up. And what the HECK? There were people with foot-long cameras taking pictures! When did they get here? I also just noticed that there were guards at every door. When did they slip in? I eyed those cameras. . . . They were going to capture me up close and personal. I'm not vain, I'm really, truly not. But those cameras could probably see up into my brain!

The duo boys were explaining their fundraising idea, which they named Pitch in a Penny. They were talking over each other and teasing each other, making the prince burst out laughing. Shy Boy was holding up his lanyard now, looking at the flash of color that dangled from it. I glanced over. It was a bird. Blue. A blue bird. I thought of blue jays. Of how I'd ended up here, right now, with an idea that wasn't half-bad, which Mrs. V and Miss Gertie and Sky and the prince of England were waiting to hear about.

So how could I NOT go up there!?! I had to just go up there. I'd be madder at myself later for not going up there. *This* was something straight out of a dream. Okay, Melody—

And from the corner of my eye, I spied movement. Sky. Weaving her way down the aisle, hunched over low, low, low not to block anyone's view. "You've got this, Melody," she whispered. "Now get up there and blow us all away!" And then she was gone. And Prince William was waving me up.

Me. Melody. Okay, girl. Soar!

CHAPTER 49

It was like my dream, the one where I walked to the podium in the cute sashed dress. Except this was real, and yeah, I wasn't walking, but—ohh—the stage was real and the audience was full of fascinating people, and I was going to own it! Everything was being recorded. And there were cameras galore. So I'd get to show my parents and Penny and my camp friends . . . . And, uh, hello, the PRINCE was here!

No, I didn't walk to the microphone, and no, Mom and Dad weren't there, but I was surrounded by folks who knew me and loved me and cared for me. Mrs. V.

Miss Gertie. Sky. And my new friend, Bethany, and my workshop crew!

I rolled to the podium, strong and confident. I wore my new silky, dusky-blue dress, which swished lightly just above my knees. A sash was cinched around my waist. Kitten-heeled black sandals decorated my feet. I straightened my back, rolled my chair to face the prince, and bowed my head. I don't know where that came from, but it's what I did. And he smiled; his eyes smiled! As he introduced me, I spied a lanyard in his hand.

I could hear people clapping, and shouts and cheers. Had to be my crew!

"You're the best, Melody!"

"You rock, Melody!"

"Go, Melody!"

And a super-high finger whistle for far too long. Had to be one of the duo boys!

I adjusted the speaker on Elvira, grateful to Mrs. Chilvers for synching Elvira's Bluetooth with the auditorium's speakers ahead of time; like I said, they think of everything! And I was ready at last. I took a deep breath and pushed play.

CHAPTER 50

Hi! My name is Melody, and I cannot talk. But I have lots to say. I am speaking to you through an electronic speaking device that I call Elvira. It didn't even exist fifty years ago. You should be glad, because listening to me without it is just plain awful.

Trust me, I'd much rather be speaking to you in my real voice—but even my parents don't know what that sounds like. I've decided it's like Beyoncé's.

Everyone laughed.

But please don't feel sorry for me. I am here today to speak for anybody whose voice is silent.

That's how I came up with my idea for what I call Fast

Blast—a device that sends a signal to 911 if you fall and can't communicate, and simultaneously emits a loud, shrieking siren to alert anyone anywhere close by that there's an emergency. After witnessing a near-tragedy, I wanted to to help those in the worst trouble, those who can't speak at all, have a way to communicate to the world that they need immediate assistance.

When I was little, I was thirsty for words, but nobody knew how to turn on the faucet of speech for me. Talk about frustrating!

And now, here I am in front of all my cool, new international friends to give a speech, and I still can't utter one single word!

I paused to nod at the audience, then smile at the prince.

Sooo, I thought a long time about what words of wisdom I can offer to you today. Here they are:

Courtesy. Dignity. Integrity. Generosity. Grace.

Now, to those of you who have not fallen asleep from listening to my boring list of wisdom words, here are the real words of wisdom:

Take the time to be kind.

Feed the birds outside your window. They are inspirations because they can fly!

Say hello to strangers in the grocery store. They're hungry—be nice!

Speak to folks in wheelchairs. We are NOT invisible.

And if you're in a wheelchair, don't be afraid to greet strangers. If they're rude, run them over. Okay, just kidding on that part.

Remember: "There is a crack in everything. That's how the light gets in." Those are not my words—I'm not that wise. They were written by Leonard Cohen, one of my favorite singers. But he's right. Let's bring the light through the cracks to everyone.

I don't really know how pressing 911 on my board got me here, but this has turned into an amazing dream where I have learned that I matter. We all matter.

I felt so honored to put my handprint on the front wall out there. To join the rainbow of colors, all those hands that can hold dreams, and then turn them into reality, is something I'll never forget.

Thank you for hearing me. For seeing me. For including me. I see all of you, I see our possibilities, and I believe in our ideas. Because of my opportunity to meet all of you, to create new inventions with you, to discover new friendships, I now truly understand the power of hope, the power of ideas, but most of all, the power of our dreams!

SONG OF MELODY

Let this circle be unbroken
Let this circle be unbroken
Let the elders with us sing
Let the elders with us sing
Let the children learn the message
Let the children learn the message
Let the mighty spirits bring
Let the mighty spirits bring
All the power of the people
All the power of the people
All the dignity and pride
All the dignity and pride

Let this circle be unbroken

Let this circle be unbroken

As we clasp our hands and guide

As we clasp our hands and guide

All our voices to the heavens

All our voices to the heavens

As each hand to hand is pressed

As each hand to hand is pressed

And our love and will is strengthened

And our love and will is strengthened

And our minds and bodies blessed

And our minds and bodies blessed

By the power of the ancients

By the power of the ancients

And the wisdom of the winds

And the wisdom of the winds

Let this circle be unbroken

Let this circle be unbroken

For this circle never ends.

For this circle never ends.

ACKNOWLEDGMENTS

Catherine Mills, who adored her Tropicana roses

Vick Mills, who adored Catherine

Cat Denton, my "ride and fly" in London,
who makes me look smart on the internet!

Rolisa Tutwyler, who guides me through rooms and Zooms

AJ Colts, who helps me understand teen boys

Phoebe-Rae Taylor, who *rocked* the role of Melody in the movie

Barbara Parks-Lee, who I met in an airport
and gained as a forever friend

Sara Holbrook was "in the room when it happened" and
who understands it all

Bethany Ballet, who dances through it—on wheels!

Jeannie Ng and Valerie Shea and Elizabeth Blake-Linn,
Justin Chanda, Michelle Leo, Lisa Moraleda, Amy Beaudoin,
Anne Zafian, Miloni Vora, and my entire Simon & Schuster family

Deb Sfetsios-Conover, for giving Melody the covers she dreamed of

Caitlyn Dlouhy—my muse, my friend, my warrior,
my British brain stem, my guiding compass

SHARON M. DRAPER is a three-time *New York Times* bestselling author and a recipient of the Margaret A. Edwards Award honoring her significant and lasting contribution to writing for teens. She has received the Coretta Scott King Book Award for both *Copper Sun* and *Forged by Fire* and was awarded the Charlotte Huck Award for *Stella by Starlight*. Her novels *Out of My Mind*, which has won multiple awards; *Out of My Heart*; and *Blended* have been *New York Times* bestsellers. She taught high school English for twenty-five years and was named national teacher of the year. She lives in Florida. Visit her at sharondraper.com.